Idiot

C000176111

C]

Cover art by Oscar Fenner

To Mr William Henry Beveridge

Squatter carry on

I was living in the dole-drums, Manchester, when I met Liz.

It happened in the dingy basement of the Cyprus Tavern where I was sitting in for a band. Their usual drummer had gone missing the day before, and since I didn't know any of their songs, I was improvising furiously. So furiously that a stick flipped out of my grip and rolled off the stage.

Liz stepped calmly out from among the small, indifferent audience, picked it up, climbed on stage, and handed it back to me. She spent the rest of the set sitting next to me on an amplifier.

Afterwards she dragged me to the bar and stood there, sizing me up.

I did the same. She had on a shabby white suit with a bootlace tie, and sported a Tony Curtis quiff.

"That was really terrible," she said. "Listen, I'm going to London to start a proper band. I'll sing and you can play the drums. It'll be great."

"Even though I'm so terrible?"

"Maybe because. Anyway, what have you got to lose?"

She had a point.

So we went.

Thus began our search for somewhere to live. We wandered furtively for several days, toting a tool bag too small to adequately conceal a jemmy, until we discovered Rotherhithe.

Dockland, squatland, nineteen eighty-four.

We eventually crowbarred our way into a forsaken council flat, and sat, surrounded by empty cans and cat litter, on an abandoned mattress on the living room floor.

"Where do we start?" asked Liz.

"There must be a local."

So we walked beside the Thames, down streets darkened by empty warehouses, Pacific, Trinity, King and Queen wharves, thick strips of plastic flapping in redundant loading bays.

The council estates were almost all squatted. On one block someone had sprayed 'SQUITTERS DIE!'

"Lucky I'm constipated," murmured Liz.

We passed a car with a smashed window, taped over with a piece of cardboard on which was scrawled 'radio nicked, nothing else worth stealing'.

Liz surveyed the scene.

"Yeah, has potential."

I wasn't so sure. The few pubs we had passed were closed, and I was on the point of chucking it in.

Then we turned a corner and beheld 'The Hope.'

The painted sign, a faded ray of sun breaking through grey clouds, groaned on rusty hinges, and there were boards on the windows. But the door was open.

Inside, a few people sat in the gloom surrounded by dogs. Liz, at twenty-nine, was probably the oldest person in the joint. A kohl-eyed female smiled over at us from behind the bar, and we bought pints of bitter and sat on tall rickety stools.

A man with tatty ginger dreads, wearing a knitted jumper that hung below his knees, suddenly got up and smashed a chair, throwing the bits onto the fire.

"Declan, don't be such an idiot will you?" said the woman who had served us.

"It's so fucking cold in here," explained Declan.

Liz smiled at me, drinking her beer quickly.

"The Hope," she said.

"Abandon all who enter here," said the barmaid, whose name was Jayne. "Don't worry, I'm only looking after the place. It's a dive. The manager's setting up a wine bar in London."

"We're just Irish peasants!" shouted the fire-tender.

"Don't mind Declan," she told us. "He's just the local do it all, know it all."

"Today I'm a heating technician," said Declan, stretching out his thin legs before the now barely burning fire.

Jayne forced a smile.

"Are you living round here?" she asked.

"We're on the Lavender," I replied.

"The Lavender! Jesus, some of them flats have electricity!"

We weren't sure if she was joking, but we kept quiet about our television and gas cooker, appliances enjoyed free due to coin meters broken by previous inhabitants.

I looked around the dark pub, a pall of smoke hanging above the worn, cigarette-trodden carpet. Jayne glanced over, half-heartedly wiping a table.

"Second thoughts?" asked Liz.

I'd moved away from somewhere I'd lived for years, with someone I'd known for weeks.

"Not really."

She smiled, and found enough change in her pocket for another round.

"Trust me, Billy, it's going to be great," she said, lighting a cigarette. Jayne winked, handing me my pint, and as I took a few sips, it seemed perfectly feasible that it might be.

The Max Factor

Within a few weeks, it became clear that Liz's plan to become the next Chrissie Hynde was not the limit of her ambition. She started free-lancing, and was often out reviewing bands or doing interviews. This spirit of enterprise on her part seemed to sap mine, and I either sat about doing nothing, or pissed away my hardly earned cash in various dives such as the Hope.

It was here that I met Ted, a singer/bass player, who was looking for a drummer to complete his line up.

"Sound!" he said, when I agreed to join. "I'll sort out rehearsal space and let you know."

Regarding our Riviera squat, though there was no damp, as such, the broken gutters sent rainwater cascading down the walls. It soaked through and caused the wallpaper to swell in great musty, patterned mushrooms. One wet afternoon, Liz stuck her finger in one of them, starting a little unnatural spring that drizzled for days.

"Ooh look, eau de source!" exclaimed Max. "We should bottle it."

Max had come as something of a surprise.

When we first moved in, we'd noticed some furniture in the small bedroom, but it had never occurred to us that someone might still be using it.

He arrived late one night, very drunk, laughing and cursing as he tried his key in the lock we had changed. Liz was out, and I eventually decided to open the door.

He stood tall in a trench coat, swaying slightly, peering at me with small dark eyes that looked down his long, narrow nose.

"Hello, hello," he said, sniggering. "Who's been sleeping in *my* bed?"

It didn't seem to bother him in the slightest that he had acquired flat-mates. In fact, it appeared to amuse him.

"Welcome, Billy, to rotten row," he slurred. "I'd ask you to make yourself at home, but it looks like you already have. What was it you said your friend's name was?"

"Liz."

"Oh yes, a girl."

Liz, initially resentful, soon relaxed around Max. They quickly related to one another in their drive to succeed.

Max was a social worker at a psychiatric hospital with plans to write a book debunking psychoanalysis, and Liz had lost none of her determination to be top of the pops. They would sit and swap aspirations.

You pat my back, I'll pat yours.

As spring wore gloomily on, I was left with plenty of time to contemplate my inaction. I was reminded of school when the little bottles of milk were handed out. I rarely felt any compulsion to jostle with the other boys and girls, often waiting until they had gone out to play before discovering if there was any milk left for me. There always was.

I was in just such a daydream-mood one morning, steam rising to my face from a cup of tea, when Liz came clattering down the uncarpeted stairs. She stood by me, picking at my eighty per cent viscose dressing gown and stealing sips of tea.

"I suppose Greta Garbo's hogging the bathroom?" she enquired, lighting an Embassy.

"I think Max is immersed, yes."

"Bye, bye hot water," she murmured, proceeding to fill several saucepans and set the flame beneath them in preparation for her turn in the tub.

"Keep an eye on those will you?" she asked, blowing smoke towards the ceiling, which I watched trail in her wake as she breezed off to find a 'phone box.

"O.k."

Steam gathered in the kitchen as I listened to Max singing, 'If I were the only girl in the world'.

"Shouldn't it be 'the only *boy*'?" I shouted.

"Not when I'm singing it dear," he called back.

Rain rolled down the window outside, condensation gathering within.

I went out onto the balcony. The courtyard was deserted, except for a couple of fighting cats. The biggest, a one-eared tabby, came off best, and wandered over to where he lived, scratching at the door. The other inhabitant was an elderly man named Vic, the last of the bona fide tenants. He rarely ventured out, and his television blared all day. His flat also exuded a smell of boiled fish, though nobody knew if he cooked for himself or his cats. One-ear continued to persistently scratch and miaow at the door, until a window opened.

"Fuck off monkey chops!" said Vic.

I went back in to the kitchen, where I found Max prancing about, barefoot, waving a box of Jaffa Cakes above his head.

"I'm not a dentist, but I know what's in this box will rot your teeth!" he gleefully announced, shaking the container and causing a few crumbs to fall on to his bald pate. Evincing no response from me, he came closer.

"Billy, Billy, where's your sense of humour?" he intoned, frowning into my face, then breaking into a grin full of chocolate smeared teeth.

"It left me."

"Oh, come on, cheer up and have a biccy!"

I accepted one, dipping it in my tea for too long and causing half to drop off and sink in the drink. I stirred the mixture, tasted it, and threw the remains in the sink, where it slowly gurgled down the plughole.

"Oh Billy, you're disgusting sometimes," said Max, flicking a fleck of sponge pulp from the corner of his mouth. Before I could reply, Liz crashed in, looking pleased with herself.

"I've got some more reviews," she announced. "And maybe an interview with New Order."

"How gruesome," remarked Max, yawning.

"Nice to be wanted," I said, not entirely sure why.

"Yeah," smiled Liz," carrying panfuls of hot water into the bathroom. "And what are you up to today?"

Everywhere was so full of steam and splashing that she didn't notice me slip outside without answering.

Thirst and Foremost

Rotherhithe waved wanly at Wapping, docklands disowned, the murky Thames lapping litter-strewn shores. I took a notion to walk under the river through the tunnel, which almost resulted in my asphyxiation. Several drivers hooted in passing, or shouted muffled gibes.

The chief attraction of Wapping seemed to be watching tourists clamber from a coach to visit what claimed to be London's oldest inn, so I decided to go back to the seclusion of Rotherhithe Street. This time I took the Tower Bridge route. The air was marginally better, changing as I crossed, blowing cool off the water, and my spirits lifted a little as sea birds circled above. I watched them for a moment as they fought over something scavenged from the riverbank, until a splash of greenish shit hit my shoes, breaking the dream.

The squat was empty when I got back, so I went straight to the Hope, where Jayne served me a pint.

"All settled in?" she asked.

I nodded.

"You'll have met Max, I suppose? I should've warned you about him, but it just didn't cross my mind. Beats me why he stays there, when he's got a job and all. Not that I'm saying there's anything wrong with your place, or anything. God, would you listen to me! I'll shut up now."

She busied herself in drying some glasses.

I went over to join Declan, who was sprawled in his favourite spot by the fire.

Jayne had told me that he was a diabetic who couldn't stop drinking, and was therefore gradually losing parts of himself.

"This week a finger, another a toe."

"You're kidding."

"Well, exaggerating a wee bit maybe."

Depressed by his condition, Declan had a tendency to seek solace in further bouts of booze.

He looked cheerful as I approached him today, though, grinning and flicking through the pages of his book. He couldn't read very well, but this didn't prevent him from enjoying 'Star Trek, the Photo' Novel'. He had leafed through it with such regularity that the pages were falling out. He replaced them as necessary, with scant regard for numerical order. This was probably why he never seemed to tire of the book. The trek always took him down a different flight path.

A few minutes after I had sat down, he noticed me.

"Hello there Billy, how're you? I'm reading my Star Trek. Your man Spock is a cool customer! I don't suppose you could get me a pint?"

We sat with our pints, and, as he collated the pages of his book, I couldn't help looking at his fingers.

He saw.

"Just call me Django, Billy, except I can't play the guitar. It's not as bad as it looks. Bit of a pain though."

He proceeded to demonstrate the difficulty he had in picking his nose with an incomplete right index finger.

"At least you can still hitch hike," I offered.

"True, Billy, true. If I was going anywhere."

We fell into an evening of steady imbibing, my bus fares saved soon spent on Declan. He was like a fixture by the fire. I wondered if it was possible he actually lived in the bar. I could imagine him, as the last customers went home, curling up by the embers like a lurcher.

"Fire's going out," said Declan, casting his eye around for fuel. "Don't worry, Billy, I won't nick your chair."

He raked over the smouldering ashes, and moved closer.

As the evening wore on, his mood seemed to change, and part way through his sixth pint he suddenly stood up, swaying slightly, swilled his remaining beer, and turned out his pockets. He cast his eye round the bar, and started shouting loudly.

"I look after the fire all night, but there's no one'll buy me a fucking pint! You'd have thought some bastard would get me a beer."

The few customers looked into their pints.

"Maybe there are no bastards in tonight," said Jayne, emptying ashtrays.

"You could put me one on the slate, Jayne, for fuck's sake."

"We don't have a slate, Declan, come on now will you?"

She put her hand on his shoulder and he went quietly out. As they passed, I thought she glanced at me from the corner of her eyes.

I sat nursing the last of my beer, raising a cloudy little whirlpool. Jayne returned to the bar, putting up towels and wiping round. She was slim and pale, with a high forehead and untidy scarlet hair, and was wearing a frayed, trailing black dress. She saw me looking, and smiled.

"What did you do to Declan?" she joked.

I walked over, noticing her sleeves were dragging in some spilled beer. She realised, quickly fumbling for a cigarette, and offering one to me. I didn't usually smoke, but it gave me a reason for staying there with her after hours.

"So, does your place have all mod cons?" she asked.

"Top of the range. I was wondering if you wanted to see what it's like in a squat with electricity?"

She laughed.

"Hold on Billy while I clear up a bit. Why don't you get some take-outs together from behind the bar?"

I woke alone, immediately feeling forlorn, like I wanted to creep backwards into the womb. Or forward to the tomb.

Long red hairs were streaked on the pillow. No sign of Liz. I obviously hadn't expected her home or I wouldn't have invited Jayne.

Liz had been stopping out increasingly, and it was dawning on me that I didn't understand what kind of relationship we had.

The recent memory of Jayne was sweet, and I was wondering how early she left when the door suddenly opened and there she was, pale bare limbs emerging from my dressing gown.

"I usually go out and get a coke to get me started, but seeing as you've the facilities for tea making…"

She offered a chipped mug.

"Thanks," I said, "I thought you'd gone."

"Not without saying Bye, Billy. I can't stay though, I've to open for eleven. Will you be coming in?"

"I might do."

"Well, I get out around three thirty, or I'm back in at five. Hope I'll see you!"

She put her almost full mug of tea on the floor, dressed, kissed me quick, and left.

I started painstakingly picking strands of her hair from the pillow.

It was dole day. A personal issue payment awaited me at the head of a queue of pensioners and prevaricators that extended out of the Post Office and on to the pavement of Jamaica road, SE16.

Wedged up, and emotionally confused, I set out on a crawl.

Towards evening, having patronised The Mayflower, The Ship, The Adam and Eve and The Neptune, I found myself mostly in the company of businessmen in a dimly lit pub somewhere in Blackfriars.

The exception to the mainly pinstriped clientele was a young woman, leaning against the jukebox, drinking what looked like orange squash. I caught the tacky fragrance of her accent, Tennessee popping in my brain, when she asked someone for a cigarette. She wore round sunglasses, hair screwed tight into little separate bumps held by coloured plastic beads, lips either sucking on a straw or surrounding an index finger as she bit her nail. She was reading a paperback, and I noticed her toes, (she was wearing flip flops), moving as if in time with the words.

Just as I decided to try talking to her, a couple of suits jumped in first, so I leaned back with my beer, listening.

"So, where are *you* from?"

"Bromley, originally."

"Right! You know you can probably get peach schnapps here. I bet you like that!"

Feeling synapses snapping, I now knew that I *had* to speak to her. I was trying to think how, when she moved suddenly out of range of her suitors, leaving them standing mid-flow, and made a bee line for my table.

"H'low," she said.

"Hello."

"Are you a new, amazing person?"

"Er, not particularly."

"Particularly. That's nice. Par-tic-u-larly. You wanna dring?"

It seemed apparent that I had been wrong about the orange squash.

She raised an eyebrow Roger Moore high, and smiled with the corner of her mouth not occupied by a cigarette.

"It's scrumpy! I *always* know what people are thinking, and drinking. Yours is a light and bitter, right?"

"Right."

I felt a childishly encouraged that she wasn't teetotal.

She introduced herself as 'Joo-lee', emphasising the syllables with a pout and a smile.

"So, English boy, d'you always drink in crappy places like this?"

"Do you?"

She sucked noisily through her straw and laughed, shaking her head.

"I just knew you would be here for me, that's all."

We became so engaged that neither of us noticed the first bell, and closing time clanged unexpectedly.

"Oh, piss on my parade!" growled Joo-lee. "No problem, I have some Southern Comfort back home. You wanna come and have some?"

Joo-lee inhabited a viable museum of kitsch toys. Robots and cars cluttered the carpet, a tin doll pouting at me through chipped enamel lipstick.

"Don't mind Mabel," said my host, pouring shots of liquor. She flopped into the only armchair, rolling her little glass between thin fingers and watching me through eyes lewdly lidded.

Without countdown she launched into a family history, and I sat smilingly assimilating her stories. The unjust closing-down of Grandpa's slaughterhouse, the incarceration in an asylum of old Ma Phillips.

Then, out came the Tarot cards.

"These, Billy, are special."

"Let's see…"

"DON'T TOUCH THOSE CARDS! You'll take away their power."

"Ah."

Her eyes on me, she shuffled the pack, slow and steady. I felt slightly dizzy, mesmerised by the movement of her fingers as she set out cards before us.

"Oh, wow!" she gasped, without further explanation, and, "Gee!"

"So, am I to be the next Buddy Rich?"

"Max Roach, please!"

"Ok, whoever. But, do you *see* anything?"

She giggled and knocked back another shot of the perfumed spirit.

"You're cool, things're cool," she drawled.

She lit a cigarette, leaned across the table, and with her free hand absently spread the remaining cards into a fan shape.

Her liquid eyes gazed loosely into mine.

"You're real nice Billy. You wanna kiss me?"

The moment tried to pass, but she blocked it, grabbing the back of my neck and pulling me to her, slight click of teeth. I noticed a trace of lipstick on hers, and wondered if I could lick it off. She started to pass her hand down the back of my shirt, and, as we slid from her chair, the needle on the record hit 'Spanish Eyes'.

A single card fell from the table and glided slowly to the carpet, landing face up. The Fool.

I left Joo-lee just as it was beginning to get light. Her last sight of me was a figure hopping on one leg, struggling with a sock.

Entering the squat, I was greeted first by the sound of Max snoring, then Liz's sleepy voice.

"Is that you, Billy?"

Quietly confirming this, I climbed the stairs. She was sitting up in the small bed, smiling hesitantly.

"Wild night?" she asked.

"Oh, pretty mild. A few too many, some party somewhere."

Her smile papered over the cracks in my story.

"Nursery school for scandal?" she mused, enigmatically.

She lit a cigarette and began to tell me about the work she had been doing. I felt envious of her progress, and wondered if she felt the same as she read between my lines. If so, she hid it well.

We sat beside one another on the bed, and the conversation grew thin. Liz kept lighting another cigarette, and commenting on how she really should try to give up. My mouth was dry. I lay down on the blanket.

Wan daylight appeared in a dishwater sky, squalls of rain hitting the window.

Liz shivered, and lay beside me with her back turned, and as the world outside woke, we started to doze in different directions.

A pink elephant in Peckham

I woke and saw that Liz had gone. She left an old envelope on which she had written, 'I've moved out, found somewhere better. Will be in touch.'

Her few possessions had certainly been removed, and I sat staring blankly at the note. There was something troubling the edge of my mind, but I was too tired and hung over to identify what.

"Billy, are you getting up? We have a problem!" called Max, his voice oddly reedy.

Stumbling downstairs, I saw him standing in the hall pointing at a gap where the electricity meter usually was.

"What have you done, Max?"

"Oh, Billy, its more a case of what the L.E.B. have done I'm afraid."

"Such as removing the meter?"

"Oui."

"Why did you let them in?"

"Oh, they said something about updating our equipment. There were two of them."

"You should have called me, made it even."

"I know, but I froze. I hate dealing with stroppy people, and they caught me off guard. And half-dressed."

As I was absorbing the fact that we were now devoid of power, I realised what it was that had been niggling me since I woke. I was supposed to be starting a temporary job. To advertise a new fast food take-away, I was to wander the pavements of Peckham wearing an elephant costume. ('Uniform supplied.')

I managed to report in almost on time.

"You'll have to do," mumbled the manager, handing me my work wear. On the back was printed, 'JUMBO PIZZA', with address and telephone.

So I was soon plodding the streets of SE15, visibility poor, swinging my trunk and trying not to fall over. People passing either pointed or crossed the street.

"Oi, Dumbo!" came a shout.

I managed to look at my watch. Nearly opening time.

"I'm sorry sir, but I'm afraid I have to ask you to leave."

"What, you don't serve elephants?"

"Not without a tie, sir."

I was getting claustrophobic. And thirsty.

A kid in a shell suit started following me, grabbing and pulling my trunk. I turned, cornered him in a shop doorway, and whispered,

"Fuck off, or I'll crush you."

He sauntered off, sneering.

Swearing at kids. I was obviously turning rogue, and the rest of the day lay before me like an arid plain.

"Hey! Whaddaya sellin', buddy?" came a drawly voice in my Indian ear. My employers' advice had been not to talk to people. Trunk-waving only. I waved.

"Hey, you're kinda familiar!" said the voice.

I thought I recognised it, and tried to focus through folds of fake fur. There stood Joo-lee, staggering slightly, a bottle of red label Thunderbird dangling from her long fingers.

Did she somehow recognise me?

"Yeah, Billy, I know what you're thinkin', remember? You wanna a dring, Billy-boy?"

She pushed the neck of the bottle against my trunk, so I removed my arm from its elephantine sleeve and reached out my hand through the zipper front, pulling the bottle inside for a surreptitious sip. The elephants' limb was left dangling like the animal had had a stroke, causing a passing child to burst into tears, its mother staring as Joo-lee groped inside my costume to retrieve the bottle.

"Why don't you change into something more comfortable?" she asked.

"What kind of animal would you be more comfortable with?"

"Ah, you know what I mean! What the fuck're you doing anyway? I can't believe this crazy elephant shit!"

"Have you never heard of the dignity of labour?"

Sitting in the corner of a pub, Joo-lee squeezing my thigh, I was wondering who would discover the cast-off elephant outfit we had left draped over a London Borough of Southwark litterbin.

"Someone'll use it", said Joo-lee. "They'll find a use for anything. One mans' poison…"

"It's meat, isn't it?"

"What, elephant? Anyhow, what's your poison?"

"You realise we're spending the wages I'm not going to earn?"

"It's OK, my daddy's rich."

"And your mum's good looking?"

"I dunno. But dad's loaded. He's a tycoon, a magnate, you know, bonds, tobacco."

She lit a Marlboro, exhaling dry smoke towards me, and drank quickly of her whisky.

"You left early, before," she remarked.

"I had animal employment, remember?"

She laughed, "Oh, yeah, you're elephant man, Jesus, Billy, you're Johnny fuckin' Merrick, man!"

She coughed through her laughter, "*I'm not an animal!*"

A video game flashed a badly animated Kung Fu fighter in a dangerous street, cutting down villains twice his size with a high kick and a flick of the wrist. The jukebox jumped on an old copy of 'Show me the way to Amarillo', hugging my pillow, hugging my pillow, and rain started to lash the windows. An old man, drunk at the bar, recognised the replacement record, 'I just called to say I love you', and began whistling a trilling accompaniment. Joo-lee, returning with further drinks, lit another cigarette and whispered effete nothings in my ear.

It was late afternoon, dusk descending, as Joo-lee and me helped one another along the wet streets around Rye Lane. We had been asked to find somewhere else to drink, the landlord objecting to what he called our 'unseemly behaviour.'

"D'you think we upset his customer?" joked Joo-lee.

Shop lights were switching off, shutters descending, as clumps of downbeat shoppers queued at bus stops, the passing traffic sending splashes of puddle water over pavement and shoe. Pigeons gathered on ledges, puffed against the cold, while clamorous colonies of starlings chattered in trees.

I stood transfixed for a moment by a neon light spangled in a puddle, headlights refracted through rain, until Joo-lee pulled my arm and we stumbled into the musty dry of another bar, carpets tacky underfoot.

I sat by the window while Joo-lee dropped coins in a fruit machine. Across the street I noticed some kids wrangling over the ownership of an elephant suit.

Joo-lee's jacket lay beside me. I picked it up and smelled damp, smoke, Paco Rabanne. She strayed over from her game, reeling a little, fiddling with the beads in her hair.

"You look sad, Billy, and I'm gettin' buzzed, we'd better go."

She pulled me by the hand, and I was easily led.

Hit by the evening air, Joo-lee soon started to sway and I had to support her. Her eyes were wide and dark in her pale face, a hand extended as if testing the darkness, cigarette precariously balanced between index and middle fingers.

"Hey Billy, h'low!" she said as if suddenly noticing me.

She tried to sit on the ground, but I fairly easily dissuaded her, and we staggered on, blind leading the blind-drunk.

Somehow, though, we arrived at her flat.

"I have auto pilot," she giggled, dropping her keys, lighter, coins.

Inside, as I felt for a light switch, I heard her retching somewhere and hoped it was over a basin.

I found her cradling the toilet bowl, from which I managed to separate her, and carried her to her room, flopping her on the bed. After pulling off her shoes, I moved her onto her side, an action somehow prompted by the recollection of seeing a copy of Jimmy Hendrix's death certificate.

Expecting to be alone for a while, I went into the living room in search of the drink I didn't need.

I hadn't been looking long when I heard her door open. There she was, leaning on the wall, eyes closed, hand held out.

"Gimme a cigarette," she gurgled, "and the booze is behind the TV."

I lit her the fag, also opening a bottle and pouring a jigger of the juice. Her eyes opened wide, and she smiled, "hey, where's mine?"

"Coming up Lazarus."

I started to fill a glass.

"Gimme the bottle, the bottle, will ya?"

She swigged like it was Evian, reanimating by the moment, inhaled smoke, laughed shakily.

"Hey, what'ya do with my shoes? Don'answer, don'answer."

She sat crossed legged, straightened her back, and took a slug from the bottle, whacking her teeth in the process.

"I really like you Billy!"

"I like you too."

"No, I do, I really do. You wanna know something, I'm psychic, telepathetic!"

"You mean…"

"What I mean, Billy, is I can *see* things. Also I can see in the dark."

"Really? And you are maybe also Morgan le Fay reincarnated?"

She frowned.

"I don't know. Why, do you think I am?"

"Search me. Maybe you're just living on a ley line or something."

"Oh, I get it, you're taking the piss, right? You shouldn't do that, Billy, it's not nice."

"Sorry."

"Yeah, well there are just certain things that come naturally to me, that's all."

"Supernaturally, don't you mean?"

"See! I knew that was coming. You're mean, mocking me."

Sixth sense and sensibility.

She put her hands on my shoulders and looked into my eyes.

"Come on then, Billy, it's obvious you want to test me, so test me."

"Ok. Seeing in the dark. Right. I'll turn out all the lights, and you can try to tell what I'm doing."

"Cool, do it!"

I did, and as my eyes adjusted, I could just begin to make out the grey shapes of objects, the outline of Joo-Lee sitting on the floor.

I lifted her tin doll.

"Hi, Mabel!" called Joo-Lee.

I dropped the doll. And my trousers.

"Oh, Billy, that is *so* juvenile. And, Jesus, do you ever wash your shorts?"

I stuck out my tongue and rolled it into a cylinder.

"Cute trick, Billy. Not everyone can do that. It's a genetic thing."

"Ok, then, how many fingers am I holding up?"

She hesitated.

"Hey, that's not really fair, holding them up behind your back! But I think it's your thumb and your pinkie."

That was enough for me.

I glanced towards the door.

"Thinkin' of leavin'?" she asked.

"Joo-lee, you're…"

"Pretty good at seeing in the dark? Not really, I'd know what you were doin' if you were in another room anyway."

She came near, so close that I could feel smoke exhaled, and see her face. Her eyes were coal-dark, pupils dilated.

The floor felt like it was slowly moving under my feet.

Joo-Lee was still staring at me. She started to giggle silently, shoulders shaking, and suddenly lunged, grabbed my arm, and sank her teeth into the back of my hand. Triggered by the sharp pain, my free hand shot out and slapped her sharply on the side of her head. She let go, drawing back.

13

"Billy…"
I was up and out as fast as I could move.

Light and better

"You know what sincerely fucks me off Billy, about losing a finger?" asked Declan one afternoon as we sat in The Hope.
"Quite a few things, I imagine"
"You imagine correctly. Life is only as good as the beer through which you're looking at it."
"You should write thoughts for the day on calendars."
"Thanks, I'll take that as an insult. See, not only am I unable to make my point verbally, I also can't point, if you see my point."
"Finish your point, and I'll get you another."
He laughed.
"Now you're talking."
He was smiling to himself when I returned from the bar.
I handed him his drink, and he raised his glass.
"Here's to the pint of no return."
"I don't think I want to drink to that."
"Really? Oh well, cheers anyway."
He sat down and examined his hand.
"The other disadvantage I have is not being able to give the old two fingered salute."
"Couldn't you do it left-handed?"
"Not the same, somehow. I'm reduced to using the middle finger, and that's American."
"You have an American middle finger?"
"Steady!"
"The Vulcan greeting is also out of the question, I suppose?"
"True! Mr Spock will have to remain a stranger."
We drank in silence for a few moments, interrupted by the early evening arrival of Max, who immediately bought a round and slumped elegantly into the scruffy upholstery of a bench.
"Hello, boys, Christ, I am ab-so-lutely knackered!" he exclaimed, knocking back his G and T.
"Fucked, actually, or rather I wouldn't mind if I was! Haven't had any for weeks!"
"Weeks," murmured Declan wistfully.
We passed the time in futile prattle, downing drinks at Max's expense. He was stale from a long stint at the hospital, 'out-psyching psychos' as he put it, but the gin was gradually relaxing him.
"You know, I'm beginning to wonder why I work at all, especially when I look at you layabouts. Someone came in the hospital last night and shot themselves in the reception area."
"Sounds painful," said Declan. " What did you do?"
"Nothing. I wasn't there actually. Horrible mess it left though, I mean some people have no consideration do they?"
"Unlike the skeleton," murmured Declan.

"Excusez-moi?" said Max.

"You know, he goes into a bar and asks for a pint of bitter and a mop."

Max patted him on the shoulder.

"I'm sure *you* know what you're talking about! Meanwhile, take this fiver and get them in will you?"

"You are too generous, Max," said Declan, snatching the note and heading for the bar.

Max turned to me, an enigmatic eyebrow raised.

"Been good, Billy?"

"Sorry?"

"Little bird tweets Billy been a naughty boy."

"No, still not with you."

"Oh, come on, Billy! Liz doesn't know if she's coming or going."

"Going, I think. You've seen her then?"

"She came by, yes. Stayed over. We had quite a long chat, actually. I think she was a bit disappointed not to see you. Not sure how things stand."

"And I am, I suppose?"

"Well, maybe not. But don't you think you're using her?"

"For what?"

"Oh, come on, these girls, Billy! I wonder whether you really care about anyone."

"No-one comes close to you, Max."

"Billy, you're simply impossible!"

"Impossibly simple."

Declan clinked drinks on our table.

"Break it up, lovebirds," he said.

Max narrowed his eyes, concentrating for a moment on his cocktail.

"I sense a story," said Declan.

Max enjoyed an audience, and would gladly fuel it for as long as it would attend him. Therefore, though we had heard most of his stuff before, we were prepared to swallow it.

"My dears, have I told you about my friend Jim, who wanted to look even more like a young Marlon Brando than he already did, had surgery, and wound up resembling an old Peter Lorre?"

Since Declan and I resisted the urge to chime in with the punch line, Max was happy to continue, and we settled.

Some time later, tanked on gin, Max turned his attention particularly to Declan.

"Still reading Star Trek?" he asked. "Good old Captain Kirk putting it about where no other man has gone?"

Declan, sensing Max to be at his turning point, avoided the goad by getting up and heading for the gents.

Max laughed.

"What's the matter, Irish? Are you unexplored country?"

Declan stalled, clenched his fists, opened them, and carried on.

Max shrugged his shoulders, and started another anecdote.

I was questioning its veracity as Declan returned

"Why the false beard though?"

"Oh, Billy, you're such a pedant."

He raised his eyebrows and took a shrewd sip.

"Declan doesn't question me, do you Deccie?"

With this he toddled off to the toilet.

"I'm going, Billy," said Declan. "I don't like the look of it. I'll come round tomorrow and have a look at your electricity."

"Sorry?"

"They cut you off, right? Well I'm the man to plug you back in."

Without further explanation, he let the door slam behind him, leaving me to the rest of Max in a pub without Jayne.

I saw nothing of Declan the next day, and also no sign of Max, last seen ambling downtown for a late one in the Ship and Whale. I spent a lonely few days broke and aimlessly wandering, which I was doing one afternoon when I spotted Declan struggling with a bicycle in Rotherhithe street. He was attempting to balance a heavy object on the cross bar.

"Ah, Billy!" he called, beckoning. "Just the man."

It transpired he was on his way to visit me, as promised, to put back the power into the premises. The object on the bike was an electricity meter.

"Put away those candles, I am your mains man Billy and shall put an end to your darkness."

I helped him with the equipment, shuffling and scraping up the stairwell and into the flat. The burden laid down, Declan sat on the floor and rolled a joint. He declined to speak until he had taken several long tokes and passed me the reefer.

"Now," he said, gesturing towards the gap in the hallway, "see them three big wires?"

"I do."

"Easy as candy, I just slot the old meter on, and while you tighten up, I'll nip down and take a look at the main fuse box. They'll have probably taken your fuse, so I'll have to double you up."

Before I could ask what he meant, he was out on the corridor knocking next door.

"In case they're in, 'cause I'll have to pull their fuse while I do the job and I don't want to disturb their telly or anything."

"That was sold long since for smack."

"Dear me, it's a scag world, Billy. Oh well, no reply today!"

With this, he trotted down to the courtyard and kicked open the door on the fuse box. I watched him as he pulled out next-door's fuse, forcing a hole in it with a screwdriver.

"Now," he shouted, "I just stick your cable in here, plug her in and it's happy ever after."

As he proceeded I noticed he was standing in a puddle.

Seconds later I heard him yell, and ran out onto the balcony.

He was beaming up at me.

"Ok Billy, try the lights."

I reached out gingerly and flicked the switch by the door. Instantly there was electric light and the buzz of a razor left on in Max's room.

"Declan, now I'm a believer."

"It's nothing. An everyday thing, like crossing the road, or…"

"Electrocuting yourself?"

"Or buying someone a pint after they've restored free power to your home."

On the way to the Hope, Declan remembered to tell me that Jayne had been asking about me. I was uncertain of the nature of his relationship with her, and reluctant to enquire. I felt there was 'history', although neither of them had alluded to anything.

I was glad to see her smiling at us as we approached the bar.

"Hello strangers," she said.

Declan noticed the fire was out and quickly busied himself with a lighter and some sticks.

Jayne pulled the pints, and I broke into my pittance from the P.O. I bought her one, and we drank to a slightly uneasy silence until Declan's sleeve briefly caught fire, and his cursing broke the mood.

"Do you want to see a film later?" asked Jayne.

Declan concentrated on moving kindling with the toe of his boot.

"What's on?"

"Thundercrack. It's at the Scala. I think it's a kind of horror film."

"Sounds cosy."

"Will you mind the bar, Declan, a few hours, and lock up?"

His eyes remained on the grate.

"If this fire takes I'll be going nowhere."

"That's settled, then," said Jayne. "I've never known you fail to start a fire."

She grabbed her bag, and we were soon bound for Kings Cross.

The Scala was a big old-fashioned cinema, a cavernous auditorium, dark and damp-smelling, which, when films were not being shown, served as a venue for gigs. Liz once almost set one up there for us, forgetting that we hadn't actually got around to forming a band.

Jayne and I sat at the front of the balcony, and she produced a hip flask that she had filled with rum at the Hope. I felt the warm nip of the spirit, and we moved closer to one another. The film opened with rain lashing vehicles on a remote highway, low budget black and white, flashes of headlights, and rolls of thunder. The obligatory old dark house of cardboard.

Jayne giggled.

"I forgot to mention, it's a sort of porno film as well as horror."

On cue, both genres collided in a scene where a woman made her own salad dressing both for and with a cucumber. A man in front of us became animated several times during the showing, his movements vigorous.

"Dirty bugger," observed Jayne.

"He's not hurting anyone."

"He'll hurt himself if he keeps that up."

She took hold of my arm, but kept her eyes on the screen.

We emerged from the Scala too late for last orders, and hurtled home on a tube train fogged with smoke.

Jayne grabbed hold of me later as we walked the deserted streets, holding me still and putting her mouth so close to my ear that I could feel her lips move as she spoke.

"I want you in my flat," she said, softly.

I stayed part of the night at Jayne's squat. It was cold and dark, just a roof, walls and mattress, but she wanted to be there. I left before dawn, pulling the blanket over her pale form.

Liz was at home, sitting smoking on the edge of the rickety camp bed.

"Why don't you let me know what you're doing, if you're ok?" she exhaled.

"I could ask you the same."

"Billy, you don't have a 'phone. What am I going to do, send carrier pigeons? You could call me."

"I didn't know if you wanted me to."

She stubbed out her cigarette.

"I might be going to America. There's somebody wants me to record some songs."

"Somebody?"

"Guitar player, song writer."

"Good, is he?"

We lay down together and when I put my arm around her she pushed it back.

"I better go," she said blankly.

Max was up early singing arias from Verdi, murdering melody. This prevented me from sleeping most of the day as I had planned.

I found him prancing barefoot on the bare boards in the living room.

"Hello, lovely boy. I have to announce that I am in love, and this time he's not going to get away!"

"That's nice."

"Oh, the enthusiasm! Won't you share my joy?"

"I'll have a go."

"I shall present him to you later; you'll be in the Hope, I suppose?"

"Most likely."

Almost certain, in fact.

The Hope was particularly quiet that evening. Even Declan was absent, and I sat at the bar with Jayne. She allowed me an occasional free drink, and, as I was telling her about Max and his mister Right, she interrupted.

"Here *is* Max," she said, "but he looks wrong."

He edged towards us with faltering steps, a cigarette, mostly consumed to ash, in the corner of his mouth. His eyes were small and red rimmed.

"Before you ask, no he didn't turn up, and yes I've been drinking. Which is what I'm going to carry on doing, and Billy's going to do it with me."

"Poor Max," said Jayne.

"Oh yes, poor old pathetic Max," he replied. "Have you ever been carefree, Billy?"

"Probably, but I don't remember."

"He doesn't remember! None of us remember! I'm so fucking tired of not remembering."

"Look forwards, eh?" suggested Jayne.

"Fucking brilliant," spat Max.

"Come on, Max," I tried.

"No, *you* come on, Billy, with your sanctimonious fucking bullshit. God! Butter wouldn't melt in your arsehole. I'm fucked off with you and your fucking cunt girls, you little fucking shit."

Declan, having just arrived, took hold of Max's ear and pulled his head towards him.

"Will you calm the fuck down, please?" he breathed.

Max smiled in his face,

"Fuck you too, bog trotter. Long live the next potato famine."

Declan started to laugh, let go of Max's ear, head butted him in the face, and turned to the bar.

"Pint of snakebite please Jayne!" he said, wiping with a grey handkerchief some specks of blood from his glasses.

"I'll get that," said Max.

Every time I wake up

Spring was still trying to be sprung, and I had been squatbound for days, self-doubt settling inside me like stale seltzer. I felt lonesome, yet couldn't bring myself to seek company.

Atrophy of the ego.

Too much of an effort even to go shopping. I was down to cream crackers and milkless tea.

"Billy, you drunken old fool," came a cry at the letterbox. "Open up or I'm gonna smash a window!"

It was Joo-lee, out of the blue, leaning on a white mountain-bike.

"How did you know where I live?"

"Oh, great to see you too! I just know things, remember?"

It was good to see her. She looked clear and blooming, hard sunlight beating through her hair, teeth braces shining.

"You look beautiful," I told her.

"Compared with you, Billy boy, I guess we all do. Here, have a swig."

She passed me a quarter of cognac, and dragged her bike into the hall, where, as bikes do, it keeled over with a crash.

"You're a saviour, Joo-lee," I said, kissing her cheek.

"Yeah, and you crucify me!"

She gave me a playful push, and then pulled me back close.

"Look, sorry about biting you," she murmured, avoiding my eyes.

"I got over it."

"Sure you did. And, know what? Not just *anyone* gets one."

She pulled another bottle from her bag.

"Port and brandy! Sit down, Billy. I knew you were in need of love and care, and I'm gonna mix us some super squash. You don't have any glasses, but I'm betting there are cups."

There were, and we were soon in them, swapping cocktail kisses and truisms.

"Life is short, Billy."

"Yes, and so am I."

"But love endures."

"It's *endurance* with me?"

"Ah, Billy! You're such a drunken fool. The world's greatest idiot!"

"You flatter me."

"You slay me."

"You're a witch."

"Let's go to bed."

She took hold tightly of my wrist.

"But we don't have long 'cause I'm taking you to a party."

Joo-lee called up the stairs,

"Don't go to sleep, Billy, we're goin' out remember?"

19

I hurried down, pulling on a t-shirt, and found her sitting on the hall floor cutting a line of speed.

"You want?" she asked, rolling a note.

"Not worth it. Can't seem to snort it down right. Too much snot."

"Thanks for the detail. Here."

She licked her finger and pressed it in the powder.

"Take a sherbet dip!"

She picked up the brandy bottle and I noticed it had bleached a ring shape into the lino where it had stood. I thought of myself, lily livered.

At a bus stop, we pushed each other around, heady in the sunset. She wouldn't tell me where we were bound, merely repeating, "we're gonna be floatin'!"

For once she was being literal. The party turned out to be on a boat.

I started getting cold feet.

"I'm not sure, I prefer parties I can walk away from."

Joo-Lee was already walking down the rickety boardwalk.

"Oh, come on, Billy. If you don't like it you can swim for it!"

I met her half way, and she popped a bitter tasting finger in my mouth, and dragged me aboard.

The minute we embarked I started to feel nauseous, and decided to stay up on deck in the breeze. Joo-Lee went below to forage for drinks and blag cigarettes.

I sat on a slatted bench that had hard clumps of chewing gum stuck under it like barnacles.

Someone joined me.

"Move up, saddo!" he said.

It took me a moment to realise it was Declan. I wasn't all that used to seeing him outside of the Hope.

He started trying to roll a joint, but the wind kept sweeping the papers up, wheeling in the sky like the ghosts of tiny suicide seagulls.

"Jayne with you?" I asked.

 "Should she be?"

He seemed unsettled, throwing an empty can in the Thames. There was a small wire litterbin beside him with a plastic notice above it reading 'wrap your refuse.' Seeing me glance at this, Declan looked straight at me, slowly shaking his head.

We remained quiet, taking turns to smoke, until Declan eventually broke the silence.

"Everyone throws stuff in," he said.

"Some people throw themselves in."

"Sure, you wouldn't last long in there, Billy."

"I wasn't thinking of me exactly."

"Nor me. I couldn't stand a watery grave. Give me burning any day."

The floating fiesta rolled down the river, Wapping, Greenwich, the suns reddish light ebbing from a cobalt sky that framed the woeful face of the man in the moon.

Declan having gone to sleep, I went below where there were people dancing, strobe lit. Joo-lee was attracting attention, mostly from men watching her move. She eyed them, head lowered, swaying to 'Everyone's a winner'.

I sat down and tried to concentrate on the view through a porthole, while Joo-lee continued her dance, a pudenda-pushing pantsula that had them on strings.

On the table, in small ballpoint scrawl, someone had written 'sex me, sex me.' I read it several times, beginning to wish I were a stronger swimmer.

The boys were still buzzing around Joo-Lee, as I got up and made my way to the toilet. 'The head', sailors called it. I felt as though mine had had helium pumped into it, nautical nausea gripping my guts as I swayed into a cubicle. I sat with my head between my knees, breathing steadily. Somebody came in and I listened to their footsteps. They stopped outside my haven, and below the metal partition I could see bare feet in flip-flops. I shot the bolt, and Joo-lee, smiling, slipped in, arms outstretched. The dark pupils of her eyes flashed wicked messages as she tried to straddle me, at which moment the boat suddenly changed course sending the two of us crashing on to the deck.

Joo-lee, lying under me, smiled up at a man standing adjusting his trousers. He was, I noticed, wearing a cap and some sort of uniform.

They could hardly keelhaul us for a bit of toilet cohabitation, so we got off pretty lightly. The chap in the cap even gave me a sort of conspiratorial nudge.

"Creep!" uttered Joo-Lee, when he was out of earshot.

As we eventually disembarked, Joo-lee tried to dance with me on the jetty, draping her arms over my shoulders, wrists dangling limply by my ears. Declan walked past us without speaking, and I made a move to acknowledge him. I thought we might have walked back together, but he continued on his way without a backward glance. Joo-lee was climbing the sky like a gas balloon, saluting the boat and walking backwards. If she had fallen in the river I wouldn't have had the energy to pull her out. I walked quickly away before it could happen.

I felt clear and sober, walking in the night air of late spring. Joo-lee, I told myself, would find her way home, she always did.

It struck me that, in some ways, I knew her better than Liz. In her out-there way, she was there for me.

With Liz and me there was so much we weren't saying.

A letter arrived one day from Ted the bass player to say we were on for a rehearsal at his place.

I went by bus with a snare drum under my arm and a pair of sticks in my back pocket. Ted's place was an untidy terraced house in Hackney. There were several mauled dog toys lying around, but no sign of the dog.

"Sound, Billy!" shouted Ted, above the distorted sound of an electric guitar.

"That's Steve," he added.

Steve nodded, guitar pick in his mouth, and carried on experimenting with his fuzz box.

Mary, keyboards, arrived late. Her face bore an expression of resignation, underlined by a permanently down turned mouth. As if to compensate, she was wearing a tartan skirt, multi coloured stripy tights, and fluorescent pink plastic sandals.

She plugged in her small Casio, and we all started fiddling with our instruments, like school kids starting a new term.

"This is promising," sighed Mary.

We wasted most of the session discussing what we should be called.

"How about 'Chairmen of the bored'?" suggested Ted.

Mary snorted.

"How about not! Since when was I a man? Let alone a chair one. I reckon we should change our name every gig."

"Oh, that would *really* help us get a following," said Steve.

"How about 'The Adults'?" I ventured.

Mary rolled her eyes.

"Is that an attempt at irony?"

She unplugged her instrument.

"Look, I couldn't give a toss what we're called. When you think of something, let me know will you? Then maybe we can write some songs."

And she was off.

Ted, Steve and me carried on the name game, and we were just re-considering 'The Skirtlifters', when there was a scratch of a key at the door, and a woman struggled in with several bags of shopping. She had scraped back streaky blonde hair, and wore snow-washed drainpipe jeans.

"What's all this?" she asked, staring at us.

"Hello, Mum," said Ted.

She looked him up and down.

"Tell me you have been to school Ted? Please to God don't let me hear you say you've been here all bloody day?"

Ted fidgeted.

"Want a hand with the shopping?"

"Never mind about the shopping…"

I slipped out. I could collect my drum another time.

Given the false start, it was surprising how quickly we progressed. I found us a derelict flat on the ground floor of my block, perfect for mum-free rehearsals. We ran an extension chord down for the amps, and stuck some egg boxes on the ceiling to deaden the noise.

Ted arrived at one afternoon session particularly chirpy.

"I've got us a gig," he announced. "Tonight, in the old ambulance station on the Old Kent Road."

We were supporting a band called 'The Butthole Surfers', who were known to augment their act with slides taken at the scene of road accidents.

We cut short our rehearsal so that we could get there in time for a few beers before going on.

"We're the Floating Adults," shouted Ted, and we launched into a short, thrashy set dominated by Steve's wall of distortion. A few bottles flew at us from the mosh pit, and Mary started spinning them back, shouting and screaming above the din. She seemed to enjoy this aspect of the performance a lot more than playing the songs, jumping and gesturing at the crowd.

Steve kept speeding up, garrotting the neck of his guitar, sweat dripping from his hair, and was the last to leave the stage amid a welter of feedback.

Backstage, the promoter gave us a don't-give-up-your-day-job smile.

"What does he know?" said Ted.

"Yeah," said Steve. "None of us has a job."

"We were pretty crap though," added Mary.

They shambled off to the bar, leaving me to dismantle my kit, and I was struggling with a wing nut when I noticed someone watching me.

Liz climbed on stage and sat on an amp. She was wearing a boy scout's scarf in place of her usual bootlace tie.

"You were pretty good," she said, with a faltering smile.

"Not really terrible?"

She laughed.

"It was strange, seeing you play again."

"We were supposed to play together."

"I know."

That wing nut was really tight.

"Well, anyway, thanks for coming. How did you hear we were playing?"

She fingered her woggle.

"Well, I'm…I'm reviewing the Surfers."

"Oh."

The nut gave in.

Mary came over and handed me a can of lager.

"Hurry up, Billy," she said, glancing at Liz. "We've got time for a few drinks, but I have to get the van back before my Dad comes off his shift, or he'll go ape."

"I'd better catch the act," said Liz, noticing the Surfers coming on stage.

"Yeah. I'd better get my stuff out the way."

She touched my cheek.

"I'll come by after I get back from New York."

Later, as I sat amongst our gear in the back of the van, listening to Mary trying to get it started, I spotted Liz through a rear window. Not waving, but hailing a taxi.

They may be drinkers, Robin, but they're also human beings!

I woke writhing and growling like some brand new kind of animal, fighting off an immediately forgotten dream. Vic's big cat, who regarded our flat as his second home, jumped on me and started kneading the blanket. His claws were sharp through the thin covers, and he knew this would force me out of bed. Tail aloft, he followed me to the kitchen where, as I tried to make coffee, he purred around me, nuzzling my calves. When I sat to drink, he stood staring at me, black slits of pupils widening and narrowing hypnotically as if to compel me trance-like to the tin opener.

"There's nothing to eat," I told him.

His austere expression implied disbelief.

"Max is your meal ticket, and he's not here."

Impassive, immobile.

"Oh, ok!"

Stepping out on to the sunblazy pavement, I checked my pockets for change. Cars were already crawling the streets, glint of chrome amid backlit swathes of exhaust in the gritty air. I stepped into the comparative gloom of a shop.

Unaccustomed to buying pet food, I was surprised by the numerous varieties. I stood mesmerised by the shelf of colourful tins, a collage of cat faces, ginger terrors, fluffy Persians, red-tongued panthers. They fawned over flavours. Tuna, liver, heart, turkey, rabbit, the choice cuts just kept coming, and I became aware of my stomach churning, coffee calling, the urge to purge. The shopkeeper eyed me suspiciously, and, realising I was sweating, I grabbed the nearest can.

Cat, of course, looked at me in such a manner as to express disapproval at the choice, and prevaricated, padding away from the bowl. He even chose to sit at my feet while I crapped, before finally taking a few grudging mouthfuls.

In the kitchen, I found some cigarettes left by Liz, and smoked without enjoyment, wondering where she was. I envisaged her in America, and, with a pang, remembered the time difference and imagined her in bed with some groovy musician.

Cat, realising he had farted, quickly left the room. Perhaps beef flavour had been a mistake.

The rest of the day I spent mostly asleep, during which I dreamed that the cigar-puffing laughter maker Groucho Marx was ordered, by a crocodile, to shave off his moustache and go directly to jail. The reptile was then seen to cry human tears.

Evening came stormily, and I pulled a bottle of Safeway premium export lager from the fridge. The label boasted a 'superb offer'. On the inside of the bottle tops, it said, were printed small images representing prizes to be claimed.

Hence, a coin meant cash, a parasol a holiday, and so on. Mine had a picture of a bottle opener.

I wondered if anyone ever won the 'dream holiday'. For that matter, what did it mean? Waking up to find the whole trip took place in bed? Why not a 'nightmare holiday'?

I obviously needed to get out, but didn't feel like the Hope. For some reason I felt wary of seeing Declan or Jayne so soon after the boat party. I thought about Joo-lee, leaving her that night to wend her lonely way. It was up to her now.

I opted to walk along the river, stringing out the time to save spending on beer, but it wasn't long before I ducked into a dive.

I was sitting in a very dark corner, drinking as slowly as possible, when I became aware that somebody was staring over at me. I concentrated on a beer mat, 'follow the bear', but could still feel the eyes on me. Then a voice, faintly familiar,

"It's Billy, isn't it?"

She walked up, smile broadening, a tall muscular woman who bore a resemblance to a girl who had been in the same year as me at school. She nodded.

"It's me, Alison Bailey, you remember!" she asserted.

Cornwallis comprehensive.

'I luv Alison Bailey', in biro, on the lid of a desk. Wasn't me.

"You can tell me to go away," she offered, pulling up a stool and sitting beside me.

"All right, go away."

"That figures. Always were an obstinate bugger, weren't you?"

"Was I?"

"I asked you out, and I never got an answer."

"When?"

"Actually, I think it was Oliver Walder, come to think of it."

"Thanks."

"I think I frightened him off 'cause I was tall."

"You got a bit of stick for that."

"Don't remind me. 'Beanpole', 'long shanks', all that crap. Well not any more."

Tired of the gibes, she had spent the last few years building her self up with weights, protein and steroids, and now called herself 'Maitresse'.

She left me to ponder this while she bought us drinks. Watching her grab attention at the bar, I recalled the girl from 5C, lanky long-socks. Black fishnet stockings had taken over.

She clicked her fingers in front of my face.

"Still a dreamer, I see." she said, downing Guinness, which she chased with rum. "Look, I'm going to a party, you can take or leave it, 'cause it'll probably be crap, but I want you to come. It's work for me, but you might have a laugh. Highbury, people with money. I'll call us a cab."

En route for N1, I tried not to think too much about what Maitresse's work might involve. She had a small suitcase with her, and was dressed in a plain black dress.

"Do you think they'll let me in?" I asked, aware of my very old scuffed up Dr Marten shoes and generally shabby attire.

"They'll do as I say," she replied.

The location was smart, a front door heavy with brass furniture opened by a young man with floppy hair wearing evening dress.

"Ah, brilliant, you must be… er, great!" he exclaimed, glancing briefly at me without comment.

Inside were men similarly dressed, and women with their hair up, high heels and puffball skirts, some dancing around handbags to the strains of Dire Straits.

"Nobody's going to say a word, Billy," whispered Maitresse in my ear. "They pay me to boss them around. Sort of a slap-a-gram. They probably think you're part of the act!"

She was shown to a bedroom 'to change', leaving me standing slightly awestruck in my Oxfam suit.

"I have Rod Stewart on compact disc," shouted our host. "The sound is am*azing*!"

It was his birthday, and he was keen to demonstrate his new Hi-Fi.

As Rod struck up with 'Baby Jane', I defected to the kitchen, clinging to the fridge like one of those novelty magnets. Inside, it was crammed with alcohol, litres of duty free rubbing shoulders with champagne.

As I poured myself a Queen sized gin and grapefruit, the sound of cheering and applause broke out in the lounge.

I moved closer to the door and observed Alison Bailey dressed head to toe in latex and chains, advancing on the birthday boy with a cat o' nine tails in her grasp.

"How like a pig you are," she growled, "BE ONE!"

He got down on all fours, squealing as she flicked at him with the whip.

"You," shouted Maitresse at a woman in a dress cut so low that it barely contained her breasts. "Ride that pig to market!"

The woman shrieked with laughter, straddling pig-boy and allowing him to parade her around the room.

Further animal-related debasement ensued throughout the evening, Maitresse in command, while I clung to the kitchen comforts.

A middle-aged, red-faced man in a tuxedo tried to engage me in conversation, but he was hard to understand. He either had a speech impediment, or was too hammered to try. I tried to nod in the right places, but it wasn't easy since he mostly seemed to be repeating,

"Munkle's viewza m-mark it w-wivapprenshun."

Then he tried to tell me a joke, roaring with laughter at the punch line.

"Y'see, y'see?" he said, jabbing me in the ribs.

After this he suddenly turned, fiddling with his fly, and hurried out.

A gaunt young man came in and mixed himself a daiquiri.

"I see you've had to suffer Matteson," he said, grinning. "Completely barking. Too fond of the old marching powder. More bloody money than sense! Now, where's that bloody prick teaser?"

I made a sandwich and stared at a hamster cage. Nothing moved. Laughter and cheering echoed in the hall, and somebody approached me from behind and placed their hands over my eyes.

"They are calling a cab for us Billy," said Maitresse, now no longer latex clad.

She took a bottle of vodka from the fridge.

"Here, stick that down your trousers and flatter yourself noone'll notice."

If anyone did, they were too polite to comment.

We zoomed through the night on the road to don't know where, me and my old classmate from the comp. She laughed, prodding the bottle in my trousers, counting her cash.

"Nice work, eh Billy?"

"Very nice. How come the careers officer never suggested it to me?"

"You're not the type. Look, do you want dropping off, or what?"

I felt too dull with spirits to make a decision.

"What."

So I crashed at the house of correction, spiralling through drink mares of customs officers in jackboots pulling bootleg bottles out of my arse.

I was on the floor when I woke, in my clothes, and the bed next to me was empty.

I drew the curtains and took in the room. Dusty, but tidy. Most of Maitresse's professional paraphernalia was stored in her wardrobe. There were several books and magazines scattered on the floor, among them titles such as 'Women's Erotic Writing', 'Venus in Furs', and 'Men in Uniform', this featuring an ego crushing photoset entitled 'Legendary Hosepipe Harrys'.

I noticed a spot of vodka remaining in a bottle on the dresser, and took a slug, swilling it around like mouthwash.

Gargling, I had a pee, splashed cold water on my face, and walked downstairs into the hall. Reaching for the latch, I found the front door to be double locked.

I stood for a moment in the silent hallway, and then quietly opened the only other door, planning to try a window. Simultaneously, a dog and an old man began furiously barking at me.

I nipped rapidly back to the upstairs flat and looked out of the bedroom window. No obvious escape route there. Small weedy gardens, back to back. I paced irritably, wondering how long Maitresse would be out.

At the front there was an open window.

Whether to bide my time or risk a broken ankle?

I was too stir crazy to stay, so I went for the jump. Perfect landing, knees bent. Unobserved, too. I struck out for the high street, and almost whistled. Then I realised I had left my jacket behind.

The situation called for a charity shop, and there turned out to be several. In front of one was a child mannequin with a calliper on his leg. Spastics Society. The inside smelled of air freshener trying to mask stale sweat. Two ladies with identical white perms and red tabards smiled at me from behind the counter.

"Anything special, dear?"

"Oh, just having a look."

"There's a lovely suit there."

It was faun.

I glanced at the bric-a-brac to see if I could add to Max's growing collection of animal-shaped crockery. He had recently returned triumphantly with a tortoise teapot. There was a cockerel pepper pot, but Max wouldn't consider anything less than a pair, so I skipped it and headed for home.

The few people who passed me walked bingo-style, eyes down, but on Blackfriars Bridge, a young man in a suit stood waving demonstratively. I assumed he wanted a cab, and walked on, but he hastened up to me. He was tall, with a large chin and a big spread of healthy front teeth.

"Dave!" he said, vigorously shaking my hand, cuff links glinting. "How the hell are you?"

"I'm, well…"

"Looking good! Like the no jacket thing. My God, how long has it been?"

"The thing is…"

"I'll tell you what, too blinking long! So what are you up to? Don't tell me, P R right? Look, we really must…shit, here's my bus! Look, give me a bell."

And he was off, leaving me holding a business card with his name on it in embossed lettering, 'financial consultant', two telephone lines.

I imagined my own card.

WILLIAM J BEDFORD
SELF DEPRECATION A SPECIALITY
(POSTAL COMMUNICATIONS ONLY)

I tossed them both in the Thames.

I was heading down towards Tooley Street, when Declan went rattling past on his bike, slamming his shoes on the road as he recognised me. He dismounted and wheeled the machine alongside.

"Max is around," he told me. "I dropped by yours but he said he hadn't seen you."

"I don't know why he stays at the squat at all, he doesn't need to."

"Maybe he gets lonely."

"Probably why he buys us drinks. I've hardly ever got him one."

Declan ignored this.

"Do you know Jayne's thinking of going back to Ireland?" he asked.

We walked on with very little to say.

Lentil illness

Max was frying liver.

"You should have some, Billy," he chirped, unusually buoyant.

"If I ate meat, I might."

"Oh, yes, I forgot you're a vegetable! It's no good for you, you'll be zinc deficient, you know?" he replied, full of good interventions.

"I get enough."

"Everything but the kitchen zinc," he smirked, tossing his liver.

"*You* used to be veggie didn't you?"

"Oh, only to keep Jim sweet, I told you about Jim didn't I?"

"The one who had his face done?"

"Oh, God, what a disaster! He's better now though, had a bit more work done. I'm seeing him actually."

"Hence the quick offal fix?"

"You are wicked and cynical, Billy. Anyway, what are you up to today, you young shirkaholic?"

I watched him eat with relish the inner organ of a pig.

What was I up to? Not much.

"Pip, pip!" he said. "People to see, places to go."

I switched on the TV, fuzzy image of a test card with dreary music, programmes for schools. 'Woman's Hour' on the radio.

I went into Max's room and looked in his socks drawer. There was a small dusting of powder in its little re-sealable plastic bag. I turned it inside out, sucking it like a sweet, went to the living room and put the stylus on 'Flat of Angles' by the Fall.

Minutes later, I almost missed the voice at the letterbox, a tentative entreaty.

It was Jayne.

"Where've you been? We've missed you."

"We?"

"Well, Declan can only stare so long at the fireplace. Have you given up the Hope?"

"I heard you might be leaving."

"I dunno, Billy. There's not much round here."

"Do you fancy the flicks?"

"The Scala!" she smiled. "It's funny, I was thinking the same, but I didn't know if you'd want to."

They were showing a bill of B-features entitled 'Four of the Worst'.

We saw 'The Projected Man', 'Monster on Campus', 'Queen of Outer Space' and 'Demons of the Swamp.'

We emerged later, slightly dazed, onto the sombre streets of Kings Cross.

"Jesus, Billy, why do the pubs have to close so early?" complained Jayne

"Can't we race over to the Hope for a late one?" I ventured.

"Nah, Bob's in. He's given me a couple of days off while he does the books. He runs things legitimate."

"Except when he's not there."

"What he doesn't see won't hurt him. But I suppose he'll fire me eventually. Maybe it would be for the best, the kick up the arse I need. Nothing else to keep me."

"Isn't there?"

She smiled with look-away eyes, took my hand and walked me to the tube.

When we arrived back, Jayne kissed me outside my block.

"I need to catch Bob before he locks up, so I'll love you and leave you."

I walked up the concrete stairwell to the squat, dropping my keys as I reached the door. As I stooped to retrieve them, it opened and I saw a pair of small feet in white plimsolls.

I looked up at Liz.

She was wearing a Greyhound bus driver's cap, smoking a cigarette and looking tanned.

"Hello Billy. I hope you're hungry."

She had brought some take-away Chinese food, which was sitting in the oven, and a bottle of Jack Daniels, which stood on the floor in front of us.

She seemed relaxed and excited, telling me tales of her trip to America.

I tried not to feel jealous of her recording sessions with 'Jules'.

She obviously felt poised for stardom, yet I was uncharitably relieved when her Walkman's batteries failed to allow her to play me the demos.

"You'll have to wait till the record comes out," she said.

"Yeah, I suppose I will."

"I better get the stuff out of the oven."

She started carefully laying out several steaming cartons on the floor.

"I'll just get the rice."

I decided to hurry to the bog before eating, and as I was peeing I heard a commotion, clattering and thumping, male and female voices raised.

I entered the hallway to see Liz, carton of rice in hand, glaring at Max who, having stumbled in drunkenly, had walked straight into our meal and was hopping around with a portion of vegetable chow mein stuck to his shoe.

"Get this shit off me," he was shouting.

Liz, about to raise her voice, expressed herself instead by slinging egg-fried rice in his face.

"Arsehole," she said quietly.

Max stopped hopping.

"Cunt!" he screamed, shaking food from his hair, and slamming his bedroom door.

"Oh well, bon appétit!" said Liz.

I looked at the squashed remains of the meal.

"There's still the drink," I ventured.

We sat down on the mattress that served as a couch, and both took a couple of shots. Hers, I noted, were pretty stiff.

"I'm going to live with Jules in the States," she murmured.

I couldn't look at her.

"Who's been at my fucking sock drawer?" shouted Max, breaking the silence.

The next morning I was sitting alone in the kitchen when Max surfaced at about eleven thirty.

"That living room is ghastly," he yawned. " I don't know what's worse, the ashtrays or the food. The fucking cat has pissed in there as well! I don't know why I took him in. Filthy animals."

He lit a cigarette and dipped a biscuit in my tea.

"Sorry about the take-out, dear, was she awfully miffed?"

"She's gone."

"Join the club, love, I've lost Jim. He hasn't left me this time, I just can't find him." He told me how Jim had taken to cross-dressing and trawling trannie bars.

"Taking too many drugs, he is, or so I was told. It's not like him. I'm not judging, Billy, I'd just like to know where he is."

He smiled cryptically to himself.

"He's not the only one who's gone a bit, you know…"

"What do you mean, Max?"

"Oh, well I wasn't going to mention it, but that little friend of yours, the American girl…"

"Yes?"

"Been admitted. Yeah, totally lost it and had to be sectioned, poor thing."

So Joo-lee was in hospital, and one of the people responsible for her rehabilitation was Max.

"Funny how things turn out," he mused, dipping again his biscuit in my tea.

Some of it fell in.

Max rallied round, as only he knew how.

In exchange for me helping him look for Jim, I was to be allowed on the locked ward where 'for her safety' Joo-lee currently resided.

Naturally, Max called in his favour first.

Pulling off his socks, he began picking his feet, and while I made more tea, he outlined his plan.

"We'll have to check out some night clubs. He'll probably be in some dodgy place making an idiot of himself."

Not as big a one as me, I thought.

"We'll have fun! I'll supply the finances while you keep me company. I don't like the sort of places Jim goes. "

"How did you ever meet him?"

"Oh, didn't I tell you? That's a long story…"

"Skip it then. When do we start?"

"You are an angel! You'll get your reward in Heaven. Well, you would if you ever went there! It will be in less salubrious nighteries, however, that we shall seek our Jimmy!"

He accepted a mug of red label.

"Shall we say this evening?"

Which was how I found myself sidling up to a venue in the Balls Pond Road, Canonbury, called the Red Hot Poker.

Hi-energy music thumped through the wall, a façade of peeling green paint coated with dust bearing a poster that read, "DROP YOUR TROUSERS, Tuesday is Trannie nite!"

Inside was dark and loud, cropped scalps and bristling moustaches flickering under flashing lights. Despite the odd floral print blouse and bouffant wig, there didn't seem to be many geezer-birds, as Declan would say.

Max had elected to remain "at HQ" for this venture and I felt a bit out of water, standing at the bar nursing an expensive whisky-and-dry, scanning the throng.

Max had informed me that if Jim were there he would most likely be sporting a blonde wig.

No sign of one yet.

'Relax!' urged Holly Johnson via a loudspeaker close to my left ear.

"Get you a drink?" asked a voice near my right.

I turned to face a small, solid man of about fifty, wearing a biker jacket, white t-shirt and a ring through his nose.

"No strings!" he added, laughing.

His voice was light and musical.

I spent most of that evening listening to Peter's life story, at least that of the last few years. We found a slightly quieter corner and, while I kept a weather eye out for Jim, I heard of a marriage, a son, evening drinking after work extending to lunchtimes, a wife taking a lover, a husband taking a bed-sit.

"Sorry, Billy," he said, drawing a love heart in lager spilled.

"No need," I replied.

I bought another round of drinks.

"I'd have got those," said Peter. "The prices they charge in here."

"It's ok," I said.

It was nice to be able to give something back, even if it was on Max.

"Chi, chin," said Peter, clinking his ring.

I told him something of Jim and Max, harbouring a slight hope he might have encountered the former in some guise. Not so, although the coincidence of the evening was that he knew 'Maitresse', who had briefly worked as an office junior at the firm of solicitors where he was a partner.

"Oh Alison, yes! Went off to pursue her other interests. She used to tell us about her exploits. We called her 'Mattress', I'm afraid, though not to her face."

I wondered if I was likely to see Mattress again, but it was Joo-lee who occupied most of my thoughts. In fact, remembering I was to visit her the next morning, I decided to cut along.

"That's a shame! The night, unlike me, is young," said Peter. "Look," he added, fumbling to remove an expensive-looking watch from his wrist, "I want you to have this."

"I can't…"

"Please, take it. There's no present like the time. Maybe when you look at it you'll spare a thought for this old bastard."

Cloud Cuckoo Land

Approaching the Maudseley hospital, I started to feel nervous in about seeing Joo-Lee. I popped into the Silver Buckle for a bracer. It was the sort of pub where drinkers barred from all the others could still get served.

Loony magnet that I am, I soon had company.

He was a Scot, a real-life red-nosed cliché, seating himself opposite me and leaning across the table with a confidential air. He wore signet rings on all his fingers.

"See," he said, "you're my pal."

I hurried my half-pint, but he was hard to ignore.

"No, see, you're my pal. You and me against the world!"

"We'll show 'em, eh?"

"Fuck off!"

"But you said I'm your…"

"I love you, son. Fuck off!"

"Yeah, well, it's been nice, but I'm spoken for."

At the hospital, somebody in reception directed me to the floor where I would find an area known as 'Red Team'. There was a glass door, reinforced with wire, and a hand-written notice, instructing visitors to ring a bell and await assistance. I pressed and, imagining a buzzer sounding somewhere within, waited. I could hear voices and laughter echoing down the corridor, but nobody came to admit me. Eventually I tapped on the glass and a man quickly emerged from an office just inside, cupping an ear as he approached.

"I've come to see Joo-lee…" I said, my voice faltering as I realised this was the only name by which I knew her.

"Fine," he replied, producing a bunch of keys.

Having let me in, he pointed vaguely down the corridor and wandered back into his office.

I followed the sound of a television blaring, and entered a common room with a lino floor and furniture upholstered in beige vinyl.

A woman wearing a pink nylon dressing gown smiled at me through a haze of cigarette smoke.

"Take the High Road," she said.

The only other occupant of the room was a middle-aged man pacing about and fiddling with the dial on a transistor radio.

I went back into the corridor, and was about to approach the office when I heard someone singing, low and slow. As I turned, Joo-lee, wrapped in a towel, came out of a bathroom. She carried on singing as she slowly approached, trailing off when she recognised me, and grabbing me by the wrist.

"C'mon, Billy," she whispered, pulling me along.

She led me into a small ward and sat on one of the four beds. Opposite her a large shape covered with blankets heaved and snored. I noticed that Joo-lee was smiling differently, as if she was not sure whether or not to show her teeth. She had made up her eyes above and below with thick swathes of mascara, and I noticed sweat beading on her forehead.

"So, what's happening, Joo-lee? How're you?"

She nodded her head, reaching for cigarettes.

"Cool, Billy, cool. No drinking, you know what I mean? A little light medication, great food, breathtaking views, all the shit."

From another part of the building I heard the sound of china being smashed.

Joo-Lee placed her face very close to mine, eyes glittering.

"Have the courage to be exceptional!" she hissed, exhaling smoke through her nose. "I realise my destiny. I'm here to help the people, Billy. I'm the me inside this form!"

She giggled.

"Russian doll, see? Doll inside doll down to the smallest, which is the invisible but most powerful."

She lit another cigarette and, seemingly confused by having two, passed the first to me.

"Man versus Superwoman, million dollar woman, catalyst woman."

"You still have the Tarot cards?"

She looked at me seriously with wide, dark eyes that I was used to seeing loppy-lidded.

"What I have I carry inside," she replied.

"Can you get out for a drink?"

She contemplated me for several silent minutes, frowningly regarding me as if we had just met.

"I can tell you one thing, one of the guys tried to fuck me."

"What? Have you told someone?"

"Not when it's one of them that did it, Billy."

"Can I do something?"

"This is my call, Billy. He comes to me, I will use him up and recycle the wrapper. I am multi-layered to the hardcore. What comes around goes to ground. Harder than you think, sooner than you think, it's ALL gonna come down!"

Dearth of a Ladies Man

Not really knowing whether I felt like laughing or crying, I proceeded directly to the nearest watering hole, and got quickly outside of a pint of 'dogbolter'.

I felt as though I had been bereaved, though Joo-lee was not so much late as lost. I started to entertain ludicrous notions of trying to spring her, but I knew she should probably stay in care until she got a better grip. I wondered if I should speak to Max about her allegation of an attempted assault, but somehow I knew I wouldn't be able to bear to enter into his confidence.

A pint appeared at my elbow, and I looked up to see Mattress, accompanied by a young man of tonsured scalp, wearing a dog collar, and a lot of stainless steel in his face.

"This is Joe," she said.

"Hi," he said, very quietly.

"Bill and I were schoolchums!"

"That's nice."

They were on their way to a party at the Elephant and Castle, and Alison said I was to join them. I explained that I was short of cash, but she waved this aside, patting Joe's pocket. It was too good to resist, especially since I had just bolted my last few coins, and had been preparing to subject myself to an evening of 'This is your life' and the like.

Joe seemed compliant, and we made an odd threesome, Maitresse setting a pace that had us trotting. Joe offered to pay the cab fare, but we were ignored every time we hailed one.

"Bastards!" shouted M, breaking into a light canter.

We joined up with a few others outside a flat that reverberated to a dub reggae bass line, and were admitted by a man who knew none of us, and, since it wasn't his party, little cared.

Clumps of people hung around the hall, billowing smoke.

"Joe, will you get us something to drink?" said M.

I could see she meant him to fetch me one too, but before I could demur, he had slipped through to the kitchen.

"He's a sweetie," she smiled. "And so are you Billy", she added, placing the tip of her index finger on my nose.

Her attention to me in front of Joe made me uneasy. He was obviously devoted to her, yet she seemed bent on confusing him. I hoped she hadn't misled him about the time I stayed over.

"Here," came Joe's voice. He offered me a can, but as I went to take it, he pulled it out of reach, hesitated, grinned, and held it out again. This time he let me have it.

I stood by the window sipping the cheap lager. The room was hazy, shapes of people dancing, a cacophony of chatter above the music. In a corner, I caught sight of a tiny blonde woman looking directly over at me. I made my across the crowded room, flicks of sweaty hair hitting my face, and stood beside her.

"Pretty crummy party," she said, in a high, tremulous voice, putting small fingers to her mouth as if afraid to release the words. She turned her head to one side and knocked back a gulp of wine, teeth magnified through the glass as it emptied. I was about to suggest a refill, when Maitresse loomed, pressing a drink against my arm.

"Wine," she shouted, ignoring the bonsai babe. "It's all that's left."

I took it, but there was nothing for the little one.

"Do you fancy another," I asked her.

With a sideways glance at Maitresse, she took the cup from my hand.

"I seem to have one," she said.

Joe was hovering. I didn't like the feel of it.

Maitresse regarded Blondie for a few seconds, before striding off. She brushed past Joe, causing him to spill beer.

"So," said my diminutive pal. "What do you do?"

That question.

"I'm a metal construction worker."

"Wow! That must be very physically demanding."

"Not really," said M, returning with another cup of wine. "Mostly just twiddling knobs and playing with big men's toys."

She held out the cup like a rattlesnake presenting its tail to an infant, and I half expected her to throw it in my face.

"I got you this Billy, as you seem to have mis*laid* the last one. Enjoy!"

She made a beeline for Joe and dragged him out to dance. He didn't look keen, and there was something increasingly unnerving about the way M enjoyed manipulating him in front of me. He kept his eye on me over M's shoulder.

I suddenly found myself asking tiny tears to leave with me.

"Can't we make a date?" she asked.

"No," I said. "It's now or never."

I didn't expect her to reply, "Come hold me tight, kiss me my darling, be mine tonight!"

And she didn't.

M strode up and took the little one's arm.

"Had enough, Emma?"

"You said it baby."

"You're a wanker, Billy," said M, as they both headed for the door.

"My love won't wait!" I shouted.

Joe cast one look back at me as he followed.

Mirth of the Fool

I was standing on the balcony thinking about the strange situation in which I had recently found myself with Maitresse and Joe.

Summer had arrived, like a mediocre cup of tea, wet and warm. The air hung around me like a damp blanket, skies heavy with impending storm.

Some boys were playing football in the courtyard. They seemed to take pleasure in trying to kick the ball against the windows and doors of the ground floor flats. This had been going on for some thirty minutes, when I heard a door being unlocked, and out rushed Vic. The old man had an air rifle in his hands, which he levelled, taking careful aim. All the boys stood still, and there was a sharp report. Vic hit his target, and grinned at the sound of escaping air.

Most of the boys ran, grabbing jumpers that had been serving as goal posts. One remained, glaring at Vic.

"You old bastard," he began, but seeing the wiry old chap cocking the gun and preparing to insert another pellet, he turned on his heel and trotted away, kicking the remains of his ball in passing.

"Morning!" Vic shouted up to me, as he re-entered his flat.

Later, as rain pelted the streets out of a deep violet sky, I hastened to the smoky sanctuary of the Hope.

Bob was behind the bar, dapper in tight stripy waistcoat and bow tie. He smiled thinly.

"And what will it be, sir?"

It was a pint.

I wasn't used to hearing 'sir' outside of school. This set me thinking about my situation, signing-on, and, supposedly, playing music. The 'Floating Adults' hadn't had any more engagements, and the last rehearsal, in Mary's flat in Bermondsey, had been curtailed by the intervention of a neighbour who worked night shifts, accompanied by a pit bull terrier that didn't.

"You really ought to think about getting a job," Max was always saying.

I did think about it, often, and it always gave me a sinking feeling in the pit of my stomach.

My dole-dreams were interrupted by the arrival of Declan, stepping into the bar with Jayne, waving as they approached. Declan had his arm around her shoulders.

"Hey, Billy!" said he, "I don't suppose you could borrow me till Thursday?"

He sat down at my table.

"It's ok," said Jayne. "I've got a few quid left."

She went to the bar.

"We went to this incredible do, said Declan. "Jesus, some friend of Jayne's works for RCA, they had this big launch party. Free food, champagne, three colours of wine, fucking excellent!"

"Pity we were thrown out," added Jayne.

"That was unjustified," asserted Declan. "I was just having a laugh."

"Not everyone shares your sense of humour, Declan. Showing your arse to Phil Collins is not universally considered the stuff of comedy."

"Phil laughed."

"But the bouncers didn't."

They lit cigarettes.

"That'll be you next, Billy, famous drummer turned solo singer," said Declan.

"I'd settle for a gig," I answered.

"There's no reason you shouldn't do it," said Jayne. "Well, the drumming bit anyway."

I wondered when she had heard me singing.

"Well, meet the gang 'cause the boys are here!" came the ringing voice of Max, some time later. He was in high spirits, leaning in the doorway and winking at Bob, who raised an index finger and levelled it at Max, mock shooting and blowing smoke from the barrel.

"I'm a girl," said Jayne.

"Who can't say no?" asked Max, fetching a round of drinks. "Now, Billy, I need your undivided."

Giving drinks to Jayne and Declan, he prised me away from our table, pulling me by my wrist to a corner seat.

"I have good news and might-be good news!" he beamed. "Your louche lady, only daughter of a very wealthy American, has been moved to private care, where she'll probably do a lot better than motel hell. At the very least, she'll get more interesting drugs…"

"Is that the good or the might-be?"

"Oh the good, *IL Buena*! I'll let you have the details and you can write to her."

"What, no visitors?"

"Oh, *sure*, if you fancy California at this time of year!"

"I see. The good old U S of A."

"Oh dear! Yes, you do rather seem to have the effect on people of compelling them to cross the pond, don't you?"

"Ha ha. What's the other news?"

"There has been a sighting!"

"Elvis?"

"None so mundane. Jim has been spotted working in a karaoke bar up town. We shall tonight, hopefully, be served by him!"

There was quite a crowd at 'Chaps', and we had some difficulty weaving our way through the thong throng to the bar. Jim did not appear to be behind it.

"It doesn't look like karaoke," I shouted.

There was a small stage, though, with shimmering silver shreds of curtains, crowned with a red neon cowboy wearing only a Stetson.

"I don't see any drag," said Max, sucking G and T through a slice of lemon.

We stood in a corner watching a few men dancing. The dress code seemed to be mainly leather and chains, some cowpokes, some bikers.

My mind wandered back to Mattress walking out with Emma. Joe's look at me as they left the party.

"Look out!" said Max, "something's starting."

Following an announcement through a silver microphone, on came the turn. He was tall, slim in a Lurex dress, feather boa and stilettos, singing 'Falling in Love Again' in a low, husky voice.

Max looked momentarily confused, as if not quite sure where he was. He glanced at the floor, and back at the stage.

"Oh my God!" he said.

After his turn, Jim came straight over to us, sans wig.

"I spotted you straight off," he said, kissing Max. "Oh, hello," he added, blowing one in my direction. "I'm not intruding I hope."

"Don't be silly," said Max.

He sounded quite meek.

"Well, love, what did you think?" asked Jim. "I've finally got over me stage fright!"

Max was shaking his head, smiling.

"You never told me you were star!"

"No autographs," said Jim, winking at me through long stuck-on lashes. "Max here is a tad prone to hyperbole."

"I'm entitled to my opinion," said Max, "and I think you're stellar."

"Mmm, 'Stella by starlight'. I don't think so. I'll stick with Lola Lamour."

"Well Max," I said, "I'd better be off."

"Thanks Billy," he said, pressing my hand. "Thanks so much."

"'Bye, Lola."

"You can call me Jim," said Jim.

"'Bye Jim."

I woke early the next morning, and found I had a bit of Max's 'expenses' money left in my pocket. I walked to Jonny's, the greasy spoon in Jamaica Road.

As I sat waiting for my order, I watched a small man in a shabby pinstriped suit being handed his 'full English'. Rashers, sausage, eggs, beans, mushrooms and a smack on the arse for a bottle of tomato sauce. Tea and two slices.

I was just looking at menus chalked above the counter, 'sausage delight' catching my eye, and 'cod royale with peas', when I noticed Mattress sitting by the window with Joe. He was staring over at me, and by unfortunate coincidence, dropped his fork when I smiled in recognition. He stood up as if about to approach, but found himself penned in behind the plastic table by M.

"What's funny?" he said, leaning forward.

"Whatever makes you laugh, I suppose," I answered, taking receipt of some scrambled eggs.

M continued implacably to masticate.

Joe stood on his chair and vaulted the table, upsetting a cup of sugar. He came over, putting his face so close to mine that I could see the slightly septic aureole of his eyebrow stud. To my surprise, he gave a slight smile.

"Will you meet me later in the Blacksmiths," he whispered. "Please?"

I could just see M in the background, craning to see what was happening. Joe's expression told me he didn't want her to know.

"Ok," I mouthed.

"Just remember, then, alright?" he said loudly, and scrambled back to his seat.

M immediately stood up, and Joe was quick to follow her outside, from where she frowned at me through the window, before striding away, Joe hastening behind.

I stuffed my grub too fast, edgy, and stepped up to pay. The girl in the nylon pinafore looked about twelve, almost translucently pale. She dropped the slip of paper and I stooped to retrieve it.

"Sorry," she said.

"Don't worry," I said, "you're not the only one who's butter-fingered today."

As she gave me my change, I noticed her glance at her hands.

Joe was not in the Blacksmiths Arms when I arrived. It had hardly been possible, at the café, to arrange a time to meet, and I wondered how long I might have wait. I would have liked to wander down to the Hope and see if Jayne was in.

I found myself looking up expectantly every time someone came in. My policy was fifteen minutes and your time is up, and I was just about to leave when Joe arrived, peering through the gloom and smoke. I had to wave before he saw me, and as he came closer I noticed he had a black eye.

"Didn't spot you," he said. "Haven't got my lenses in, bit sore."

He got himself a drink and sat opposite me.

"Thanks for this, Billy. I know you don't really know me, but I thought you might be able to help. I think Maitresse is losing it."

"The eye?"

"Oh, yeah, she gets a bit physical, I'm pretty used to that. It's just, lately, I can't seem to do anything without her getting mad. I had to lie about tonight."

"I don't know her at all really, Joe."

"She said she was at school with you."

"That was Alison Bailey. She's changed a bit."

"She said she fancied you then."

"I wouldn't have noticed."

"She doesn't now. Actually, she's started getting jealous of everyone. If she knew I was out with you…"

A little damp mascara seeped from the corner of his eye.

"She's so fucking possessive! She doesn't want me at the art college anymore. I do modelling there. Did, anyway."

"What are you supposed to be doing tonight?"

"I'm at my Uncle Mike's. He's got emphysema. I usually bring him his fags and a 'Standard'."

He picked at the label on his bottle of lager.

"She seems to hate everyone I know, and keeps on trying to persuade me to feel the same."

He slipped a strip of gum in his mouth and offered the pack.

"No thanks."

"No? Helps me relax. Maitresse hates it, says it's a annoying habit."

"Sounds to me like she's scared."

"Scared? Are we talking about the same person?"

"Well, you know, threatened. Needing to be in control. Have you talked about it?"

"That'll be the day! She says she doesn't want things to get heavy."

"Not much."

"Verbally, I mean."

"Yeah, sorry, I'm not being much help."

"You are, actually. It's good to, well, you know. I need the toilet."

He tooled off in that direction, peering myopically ahead.

I was idly attempting origami on a beer mat, when the door crashed open, and in walked Mattress, wild-eyed and leggy. She homed straight in on me, glared, and marched purposefully towards me.

Involuntarily rending in two my cardboard aeroplane, I beamed like a faulty light bulb giving its last shot before plinking.

"HELLO!" said M, as if addressing an errant child.

"Hello," I replied, in character.

"Fancy finding you here," she added, and it was pretty clear she *had* fancied it.

"Not your usual, is it?"

"Oh, you know…"

"Not sure I do, Billy, so why don't you tell me?"

"I don't really have a usual."

She stood with her hands on her hips, a lowering tower.

"I suppose you want a drink?"

I was about to reply, when I noticed Joe emerging from the gents, edging forward, wincing through the fug. So did Mattress.

"Right!" she uttered.

She seemed suddenly amazingly large, tapping long, black-varnished nails on the table. Her hair was arranged into trussed-up curls resembling coiled serpents. I looked at her reflection in my beer, and soon saw Joe's head join hers'. They observed one another for a few seconds, until M suddenly raised her hand and smacked her open palm across Joe's ear.

He shook his head, reddening.

"Maitresse," he began, but was slapped into silence.

They both seemed to be moving in slow motion.

"Come on…" I demurred.

"Keep out of it," snapped M, glaring at Joe, her lip curled in a tense smile.

He was looking at the carpet, as if about to drop to his knees, when he suddenly whipped up a fist and socked M on the jaw, jolting her head back so that she almost lost her balance.

Looking like one who has unexpectedly had a wasp land on her nose and sting it, M uncrossed her eyes and stared at Joe as if scrutinising an exhibit at a freak show.

"You utter…fuckhead," she observed. "You're *really* gonna wish you hadn't done that!"

She weaved her way out.

"It'll still be worth it," said Joe.

Snogs for Swiggin' Lovers

The thumping beat behind something by 'Dead or Alive' threatened to vibrate me out of my bed.

I went down and found Max dancing with Jim in the living room. They were both wearing only their underpants.

"Afternoon!" chirped Max, slurping from a glass held behind Jim's head, as they cavorted arm in arm.

Alerted to my presence, Jim dashed out of the room.

"You've scared him now, he's terribly shy," said Max.

"Lola, shy!"

"It's an alter-ego thing, dear."

"Tea?"

"I'll just refresh my glass I think, won't you join us?"

Jim tripped back in, wearing something silk with dragons on.

"Oh, do," he enthused. "We'll have a ball!"

They looked very contented, arms on one another's shoulders swapping drinks.

"I better not," I said.

I wanted to go to the Hope, clear headed, and see Jayne.

"Oh well," they chimed. "Toodle-ooh!"

They laughed, embracing and kissing, as I stepped out into the day.

The Hope was home to tumbleweed.

Bob leaned wearily on the bar, a cup of stale coffee at his elbow.

"I shouldn't be here," he informed me, automatically pulling a pint of best. "Jayne's left me in it, and not for the first time either."

I wasn't used to him being so conversational. Maybe it was due to the lack of custom.

"She's usually pretty reliable isn't she?" I said.

"Generally, yes, but if you throw Declan in…" he paused, lighting a slim panatella, "you run into problems."

"Really?"

"Oh yes! I sometimes wonder if he's all there."

"If you think about it, he actually isn't."

"Steady on. What I'm referring to is the mind. There's a few things I've noticed…" he trailed off as a delivery arrived and he had to open the cellar.

I sat at the bar pondering what 'things' there were to know about Declan. And Jayne.

"Did either of them mention where they were off to?" came Bob's voice, rising up the cellar steps. "Or for how long?"

"No, neither of them did," I replied, staring at the thin head on my pint.

Bob re-established himself behind his cigar and sat trying to blow smoke rings.

"You seen anything of Max?" he asked.

"Quite a bit of him," I said.

"He still, you know, friendly with what's his face?"

"Jim?"

"Yes. He still?"

"Yep."

Bob blew a long plume of smoke, which coiled in his coffee cup like a miniature tornado.

"None of my business, I suppose. Not hurting anyone."

"When did they go?" I asked, casually.

"Eh? Go?"

"Jayne and Declan."

"Oh. Not sure, but I'll tell you one thing, I got no notice. I sometimes wonder why I keep that girl on."

"Who else is going to run a place like this?"

"Steady! Mind you, it is a shit-hole. You should see my place up Vauxhall."

He stubbed out his smoke and wandered about flicking at cobwebs with a tea towel.

"Look," he laughed, "even the flipping spiders have deserted us!"

I decided to walk to a cheap supermarket for basic provisions, making my way through Southwark Park. The sickly aroma of coconut artificially sweetened the air, biscuits being baked in some nearby factory.

I thought about Joo-lee, cooling off in sunny California, Jayne and Declan, missing presumed together, Mattress and Joe, boxing like a pair of kangaroos.

Max and Jim waltzing on cotton wool clouds.

Without warning, my gut convulsed, rejected the pint I had drunk, and I spewed against the nearest tree.

I stood gulping for a moment, glancing around. At least it happened before I was in the shop, and out of sight of the people of Bermondsey.

Or so I thought, until a small girl emerged from behind the tree, where she had been sitting spearing dog turds with a stick.

"You throwed up!" she squealed, pointing me out with the shitty end.

Despite the unpleasantness en route, I found myself shimmering around among the shoddy shelves of KwikMart, tossing items into a wire basket.

I quickly scrabbled together some basics, and joined the second longest queue, experience having taught me that the shortest always moves slowest.

Except for this afternoon.

Either side of me shoppers shuffled forward, while I stood rooted, staunchly scrutinizing the appliqué pierrot clowns on the woman's cardigan in front of me.

My concentration was broken by somebody nudging me from behind with their trolley. Perhaps they thought forcing me forward would start a sort of chain reaction.

When I failed to respond, I heard a familiar voice. It was Vic, a man I imagined never ventured further than the courtyard of our block.

He indicated with a bony finger the young black woman working the aisle.

"Colour on the till," he observed, satisfied that this explained the slow progress of our queue.

Once outside, I noticed Vic had far too many bags than he could carry.

"How do you get that lot back?" I asked.

"I don't live far," he said. "Someone usually gives us hand."

As I took some of his plastic carriers, many times re-used judging by the greasy feel of the handles, I realised he had no idea I was somebody who lived on the same block as him.

"Maybe you should get one of those shopping trolleys," I suggested.

"And look like a bleedin' nancy boy? Get out of it!"

We walked slowly through the park, and I learned he had been retired from London Transport due to ill health.

"Angina," he said, grinning. "Sounds like something out of a dirty book don't it?"

We ambled home and were greeted at Vic's door by several cats. There were more inside, including the one that often lodged with Max and me.

On the stove was an enormous saucepan full of greyish liquid topped with boiled fish scum.

"We'll have a cuppa," said Vic, filling a small aluminium kettle.

There was an old armchair by the cooker, with a cushion bearing the impression of Vic's backside. He sat on it.

"No, I can't complain," he said, loosening his tie. "I've had a good little life, really. I been here nigh on twenty year. Council wanted to re-house me, but I wasn't 'aving it. No thank you."

He got up and made a very pale brew of tea.

"Sugar?" he asked, as he stirred two heaped spoonfuls into my cup.

Cats wandered and lolled about the kitchen, the mat strewn with their fur. One of them caught a fly. There were several, hovering around a plastic food bowl on the floor, landing from time to time on the drying remnants of fish.

"Biscuit?" said Vic, offering a packet with the word 'Nice' on it.

He eased himself back into his chair.

"No, no sense uprooting an old bugger my age, no bleedin' sense at all. They'll take me out of here in a box. And what about the cats? You can't go shifting them about, and I couldn't leave 'em, could I?"

As if to endorse this, one of them jumped onto his lap.

"Watch it, monkey chops," he warned, "I've got hot tea 'ere!"

He scratched the animal's chin.

"No, couldn't leave you, could we boy?"

The others slunk jealously around his legs.

"Alright, Stanley, come on Margaret, behave yourselves!"

I left him chatting with the animals.

Back home the flat was empty. So was the vodka bottle that rolled as I opened the living room door.

I put 'Rock 'n' Roll Animal' on, long guitar intro breaking through to the familiar start to 'Sweet Jane.'

I woke up at about ten, lying awkwardly in the gloom.

Straight to the Hope.

Jayne was behind the bar and Declan was hunched over a pint.

"How's things?" asked Jayne.

"Alright. Bob said you've been away."

"Oh, yeah, just a couple of days. Camping."

"Whereabouts?"

"Lake District," said Declan. "Rained the whole time. No wonder there's so many big fucking puddles."

He brought his glass over for a re-fill.

"All there is up there are hikers and dead fucking sheep," he complained.

"You are *such* a misery guts!" said Jayne.

"If it hadn't been for the blow I'd have gone mad," he replied.

"Well you wouldn't have had far to go."

He took his pint without comment and sat down with his back to us.

"You try and do him a favour, do something nice for him…" said Jayne.

She looked sad and distant.

"I've got a tent somewhere," I said.

"We'll have to go some time," she answered.

"I wouldn't fucking bother," murmured Declan.

At midnight the three of us were still in the pub. Jayne had stopped bothering to take any money at around closing time, and there were no other customers. Declan had fallen asleep at eleven.

"Can you help me get him home?" asked Jayne.

As we dragged him along, I realised I had no idea where he lived.

"He sort of dosses here and there," Jayne told me. "Sometimes he stops at mine. I'm surprised he hasn't descended on you."

This evening we dropped him at a flat on Albion Street. It was quite an effort moving him and I wondered if Jayne had ever tried it alone. The door was opened by a huge man with a spider web tattoo on his bald head.

"Thanks for sorting him out," he said, his voice unexpectedly high.

He put Declan over his shoulder and carried him through to a couch.

"I won't ask you in 'cause I have to get to kip," he called out.

I shut the door and we walked back to my place.

"Do you want to stay?" I asked.

"Anything's better than a leaky tent with Declan," she said.

I think she was joking.

During the night I was woken by Jayne moaning in her sleep, "Declan, get your hands off my underwear!"

"Billy," came Max's voice, wrenching me out of sleep.

Tapping the door with his fingernails, he pushed in.

"Oops, sorry, didn't know you had company!" he chirped.

Jayne was still asleep.

Max smiled coyly.

"You'll never guess what I've seen," he said. "There are *huge* posters of Liz around town advertising her debut single!"

He paused to sip tea.

"Oh and I heard some people down the street actually got put in *prison* for cheating the L.E.B. Not to mention the talk of imminent evictions in the area. Oh well, just thought I'd say, must dash, ta-rah!"

Reasons to be tearful, one two three.

Life sometimes seemed just too ridiculous to go on living.

Nevertheless, I got up out of bed, shaved, looked at the top of Jayne's head, the rest of her swaddled in sheets, and walked to the job centre.

That dreary edifice, within which labour was exchanged, stood on Brunel Road.

I entered and hopelessly started reading the cards.

Most of the jobs were so basic even I was over qualified for them. I'd have to play down my exam results, and exaggerate, that is to say invent, my work experience to even stand a chance.

I picked a card offering a porters job at the Throat Nose and Ear Hospital, Kings Cross. Shuddering at the thought of early shifts, I took it to a man behind a desk, upon which he placed it, aligning its' edge with that of his blotter. He glanced at me briefly before reading the text.

"Have you done this sort of thing before?" he enquired.

"More or less," I said.

"I see. And you would now like to do rather more than less?"

I nodded, feeling like I was already undergoing the interview that he now proceeded to arrange for me.

Replacing the telephone on its receiver, he pushed the card across his desk towards me, tapping it with his index finger.

"You have to make an effort with your appearance, you know?" he said, eyes on the card.

His tapping finger was nicotine orange.

"Yes, I know," I replied, taking the card and replacing it on the board before leaving. Feeling like I had already failed, I walked along the path, running through my mind several alternative replies I might have given to the job man. They were not subtle. Quite inventive though. I started trying a few out loud.

"First sign of madness, Billy," said Jayne.

"Oh, hello. Didn't see you there."

"Well I was rather hoping the 'badly shaved baboon' remark wasn't meant for me. Someone rattled your cage?"

"I belong in one."

"*Behind* bars, you mean, instead of propping them up? I'd visit you."

"But would you wait?"

"Sure. Yellow ribbons at the ready."

"My colour."

We walked towards the river, past Hope (Sufferance) Wharf and the Church of St Mary the Virgin.

"Do you believe in our lady?" asked Jayne.

For a moment I thought she meant her mother, and was about to deliver an apparently surreal reply when I realised she was gazing at an icon of Mary.

"Do I believe? I don't know, I think the virgin birth is stretching it a bit."

"Billy, that's awful!" she said, tweaking my ear. "Seriously, though, what's it all about, d'you think?"

"I think it's about being alive, then being dead."

"So what's the point of it?"

"Does there have to be one?"

"I don't know. There must be some reason we're here."

"Probably because we're not somewhere else."

We stopped by an installation of oversized ropes fashioned to exemplify various nautical knots. Jayne jumped up onto one of them.

"Is this what you call a sheep shank?" she asked.

"Now that's something you can believe in."

"Then, how about a sheepish shag?"

I couldn't think of an answer.

Jayne smoked a cigarette, and was just lighting another from the butt of the first, when there came a clattering at her rickety front door.

Declan's teeth appeared at the letterbox.

"Jayne, are you in? Show me your fucking face!"

"Grimacious!" remarked Jayne. "Pissed again." She jumped into a pair of knickers and walked towards the door.

"Aw, cm-on Jayne, I need to fucking talk with you!"

"I'll let you in if you're going to be ok."

"Ok? O-fucking-k? Cm-on, Jaynee!"

"Billy's here."

"So what? 'Billy's here!' What the fuck is that supposed to mean?"

From the bathroom, to where I had repaired for a piss, I heard the sound of the door being opened. The flush wouldn't work, and I emerged guiltily to face a delirious Declan coming towards me. His arms were outstretched as if he intended to embrace me, yet I was surprised, nonetheless, when he did, putting his face very close to mine and gripping the back of my collar.

"I love her, Billy," he said hoarsely.

I noticed a shred of tobacco quivering on his lower lip, and realised he was crying, tears rolling, sobs shaking his thin frame.

Jayne, approaching, made one of those soft sounds reserved for such situations, and wrapped her arms around the two of us in a huddle worthy of The Waltons.

In the squeeze, my face became nestled into Declan's left armpit. There was a distinct aroma of Old Spice, and I wondered if he shaved there.

"Jesus, God," he uttered.

"It's ok," said Jayne.

I couldn't think of anything to say or do, and therefore didn't. The three of us remained clinched, Declan snotty and tearful, Jayne biting her lip and offering him a bit of tissue which he drenched and dropped.

"Maybe if you go, sweetie," said Jayne, gaining eye contact with me behind Declan's back.

It seemed the most sensible way forward, though I was aware of conflicting emotions, curiosity, sympathy, jealousy and sadness.

"Billy," said Declan, suddenly sober and snivel-free. "I don't have any claims, but if you could give us some space?"

Travelling time.

I released myself from the scrum and slipped out the door without looking back.

Dopey

I awoke one morning to find myself transformed into an enormous teenage mutant ninja turtle.

Then I woke up.

A strange noise had roused me, some sort of crashing sound from the kitchen. Breaking glass.

I edged down the stairs, concentrating so hard on being quiet and stealthy that I almost fell into the hole where the two lower steps were missing. Previous tenants had smashed them in the hope of making the flat less habitable to squatters. At least they hadn't poured concrete down the toilet, or ripped out the sockets.

No further sound from the kitchen. Maybe the cat had knocked something over. But also the window looked directly onto the balcony, and had always seemed to me to be an easy way in.

I moved slowly towards the door, just as another crash echoed out. If there was somebody in there, I didn't want to corner them.

The best thing, I decided, was to go out onto the balcony and try to find out what was happening by looking through the kitchen window. While I was doing so, a mischievous gust of wind slammed shut the front door.

Ten thirty a.m. I was locked outside wearing a pair of red pyjamas patterned with cartoon mice wearing boxing gloves.

I peered through the dirty panes into the kitchen. There was broken glass on the ledge, but no smashed window. I remedied this by breaking a small pane near the catch, reaching in to open the window just as a neighbour emerged from next door.

"Want a hand up, mate?" he asked.

I declined and he shuffled off without a backward glance.

I climbed in, treading gingerly among shards of glass. There was an aroma of yeast, and then I realised.

I recalled Max's home brewing advice.

"Of course it's ready to bottle. And put twice the amount of sugar in, it'll be stronger."

The bottles that had not yet burst stood ominously on a shelf, each one a pint-sized time bomb, and it was up to me to dispose of them.

It was an unusually warm morning, and those up and about regarded with curiosity the spectacle of a person clad in an overcoat, scarf wrapped about his head, dark glasses and gloves, carrying at arms length bottle after bottle and pitching them over the balcony.

"It's the invisible man!" someone shouted.

I wished I was.

Cursing Max, I continued with the controlled explosions. The pressure in one bottle popped the cap as I carried it, sending the pent up ale above my head, where it hung for a moment like a swarm of bees, before descending upon me in one great aromatic splosh.

Mission accomplished, I dived inside and began peeling off my sticky, sweaty garments. The patter of light applause alerted me to the presence of Max leaning in his doorway, his face taut with pleasure.

I was walking, again, aimless.

Passing a shop called 'Mr Cheap Shoes', ('the very, very cheap footwear man'), I hit a run of punning fascias. 'Use your loaf', a bakers, 'The Mane Event', hairdressers, 'Shoe-permarket', more shoes.

Shops seemed to pass in and out of fashion before my eyes, ranging from the predictable, 'Brush Strokes', D.I.Y, to the surreal, 'Percy's Freshness', a greengrocer's. 'Landlord Cleaning Services.' Is your landlord in need of a wash?

It was a wet day, and I of course managed to step on one of those loose paving slabs that lie waiting to disgorge a load of dirty water over your shoes.

My preoccupations were stemmed by a pleading voice asking if I had twenty pence.

A very thin woman, about thirty was looking directly into my eyes.

"I'm tryin' to get the bus fare."

She had a number two haircut with a zero back and sides.

I fumbled for change, and felt a hand stop mine.

"Will you walk with me a bit?" she asked. Her eyes were green, with specks of gold.

"I'm not really getting a bus," she admitted. "It's what I tell people to raise a bit of cash. I'm Madeleine."

We went into a café and sat by the big steamed up window that gave a hazy picture of people passing by.

She rolled a stringy reefer of pure grass and lit up.

"You're quite uninhibited," I observed.

"You're not," she smiled.

A man eating liver and mashed potatoes wafted a hand in front of his nose, which crinkled as smoke trailed under it. He shook his head, muttering.

Madeleine gave him a little wave, and laughed.

"One may legally smoke a pipe, or some foul smelling cigar, but this is a criminal offence. How shit is that?"

She laughed, took a long drag, and offered the roll-up. I declined, sticking to tea.

"Hey ho," she said.

We walked out together.

"Where do you want to go?" I asked.

"Do you have a schedule?"

"No. I was just wondering."

"If I would fuck you?"

"No. Not really."

"We could go to your place."

"Well…"

She kissed me suddenly, smothering my words.

"It could be nice," she whispered. She smelled of something I recognised but couldn't put a name to.

I bought a bottle of cheap red on the way. Madeleine didn't drink, so she poured one for me. I was sitting with my back to the wall. She handed me the cup, stood in front of me, smiled, took two bunched handfuls of her long dress, and pulled it up over her face, spreading it above her head like the raised tail feathers of a peacock. Apart from a thin ankle chain she was now naked from the neck down.. Her hipbones jutted, bookends to the narrow strip of her silky, almost straight pubic hair.

"I'm part Chinese," she told me, her voice slightly muffled under the dress. I swallowed harsh wine. She stepped closer, rocking on the balls of her feet. Her naval was almost touching my nose.

The front door slammed, Madeleine dropped her dress, and Max burst into the room.

"Oh Billy, oh Billy oh baby," he sang, then, noticing Madeleine, "oh, sorry!"

"Nice timing," I remarked.

Madeleine sat down and started rolling one of her tight ones.

"I can make myself scarce," said Max, picking up the wine bottle and examining the label. "Hate to be a gooseberry! God, Billy, how can you drink this plonk?"

"You want some?"

"Thought you'd never ask. I'm Max, by the way. Billy has no manners." He limply shook her hand. " Is that patchouli I can smell?"

"I'm Madeleine, and, yes, it is."

"God, haven't whiffed that for years. Oh, Billy, this wine really is Vino Collapso."

Madeleine waved the joint at him.

"Why not? Might improve the taste of the wine," he smirked.

It transpired that Madeleine was a postgraduate doing a PHD in sociology.

"It's why I was out begging," she told us. "I'm trying to get a feel of genuine poverty, homelessness."

"Oh *yeah*," nodded Max, exhaling smoke, "you have to really live it, you know, get close to the subject."

"Abso*lutely*!"

I went for a piss, and decided not to go back. I lay on my bed, drifting off to the drone of Max and Madeleine.

"I mean you can go to all the lectures you like…"

"So right! I mean the best teacher is the street…"

"…no substitute…"

Where was Joo-Lee when I needed her?

I am sitting behind a beautiful drum kit, fresh skins, brand new cymbals, and the band is all tuned up and ready to play to a large, expectant audience. Spotlights come on, bright and hot, there is applause, and the singer smiles back at me. It's Liz.

And then I realize I have NO drumsticks.

I woke at some grey hour and got a sudden snapshot of Madeleine's taut thighs.

I crept downstairs, but, apart from the lingering odour of marijuana, the front room was empty. For some reason, I also looked in Max's room, very carefully turning the door handle. He was asleep on his back, mouth open, lightly snoring. Alone.

Gainful

"You have post!" called Max one morning, standing at the bottom of the stairs.

Jim's head appeared from their room at the same time as I emerged from mine.

"Not you, silly," said Max, furrowing his brow at Jim. "They're for our lovely lothario."

He handed me a post card and a brown envelope. The sight of the latter flipped my stomach as I had been having a disagreement with the Inland Revenue.

But it was from the personnel department of the Throat Nose and Ear hospital, where I had recently attended an interview. I read, with a not entirely unpleasant feeling of shock, that I had been successful in my application 'for the post'.

To the accompaniment of congratulatory noises from Max and Jim, I then read the post card, which was from Joo-lee.

"Hey billy, I'm far out and far away how are you I'm better. Wish you were here but no gentleman visitors!! Look out London town coz I'm coming back some day come what may they are getting me straight. MISS U!!!XxxX"

This the only news from the States. Nothing from Liz. Her record had come out and gone, (I never heard it), and the posters of her face had been pasted over with someone else's.

"You've only gone and got a *job*!" remarked Max.

"Good for you Billy," said Jim. "You'll be able to get yourself out of this dump before long."

"Yes, well, I suppose no-one *would* really live here permanently by *choice*," murmured Max.

He was probably right. A new job, actually my first, and new people.

It ought to feel good.

"This calls for a celebratory drinky," said Max.

"Like you need an excuse," smiled Jim.

"Miaow! How about it, Billy, lunchtime at the Hope?"

I was trying to avoid the place, leaving Jayne and Declan to get sorted, if that was what they were doing.

"I'll tell you what, much better idea," said Jim. "You can come with Max tonight and we'll have drinks after my turn."

He was appearing as Lola in a club in town, 'The Performing Ferret'.

We arrived early, no other customers there, and sat at the quiet bar, three unwise monkeys on stools.

"I'll have to start getting ready in a mo.," said Jim. "You wouldn't believe how long it takes me to get my face on."

"Oh, I think I would," Max replied. "Have another gin and it first."

"No more than one before a show, I've told you before. Ruins my timing."

He got up, kissed me on the cheek while winking at Max, and went backstage with his little suitcase.

"Break a leg," called Max.

He looked around the club.

"Ooh, look," he remarked, pointing at a poster, " there's another act on before Jim, I mean Lola!"

I read it.

'Tonite! Lola Lamour, with support from Long Dong Silver.'

"Now that kind of support he doesn't need," observed Max, "Honestly, no class at all, I don't know why he plays these places."

"He's not exactly beating off the offers is he?"

"His career is progressing in a satisfactorily upwardly mobile fashion, thank you very much."

He bought us drinks, and we sipped and watched. The gathering clientele were generally middle-aged men, a couple of blatant trannies in floral print dresses and brash wigs, the ubiquitous denim and plaid.

Max seemed more happy and relaxed than I could remember seeing him.

"I'm crazy about him Billy," he said, gazing into his drink.

A flurry of applause and whistling broke out, and we looked towards the stage where Mr Silver had made his entrance. The latter's act involved him gradually removing a rudimentary pirate's costume while dancing to 'Frigging in the Rigging', as rendered by certain members of the Sex Pistols. His manoeuvres were neither subtle nor coordinated, and his piece de resistance was drawing a long rubber dildo from a scabbard at his belt and dipping it in the drinks of those spectators lucky enough to be sitting near the stage.

"Thank Christ we're out of range," remarked Max.

I nodded.

"You don't know where it's been," he added. "Talk about gilding the willy!"

Sparse applause accompanied the naked figure vacating the arena some moments later.

"Where's his parrot?" smirked Max.

The reception for Lola was noticeably warmer, and not just from Max and me.

"He's got talent, Billy, talent," whispered Max, gazing upon his befrocked partner.

Jim-as-Lola opened with 'Hey Big Spender', and was just going into 'Perhaps, perhaps, perhaps', when I felt somebody tapping my shoulder.

"Got the time?" he asked, laughing. It was Peter, who had given me his watch that evening at the 'Red Hot Poker.'

We moved to a corner table.

"People will get ideas if you keep being seen in joints like these," he said. "Are you still helping your friend look for his?"

"We found him. That's him up there."

"Not Lola? Well, bloody hell! I'm a fan, been watching her from her first gigs. If I'd known, I might've helped you before, but your description didn't mention certain attributes."

"We didn't realise Jim possessed them."

I noticed Max shooting arch glances towards us, so I waved him over.

"Isn't she marvellous?" he trilled.

Peter smiled shyly.

"Better all the time."

When Lola had finished her encore, she joined us.

Max raised an eyebrow that begged introductions. These done, I was treated to an adoring exchange of compliments regarding Lola's art. She beamed at us, sweat breaking out on her forehead.

Close-up, the makeup was less effective, some of the lines on Jim's brow creasing the dry pancake, his teeth appearing yellowish.

He kissed Max on the cheek, leaving a lipstick print, and smiled at Peter.

"I've seen you before, haven't I?"

Peter gazed into his lager, lost for words.

"Your friend is bashful," said Max.

"Leave him alone," said Jim, slightly snappy. "He's very sweet. My greatest fan!"

"At least you didn't say 'biggest'," murmured Peter.

"I think drinks would be nice, don't you," averred Max, slipping some folding into my palm. Having been adopted as the gofer, and having only empty pockets with which to object, I made my way to the bar.

Max was evidently delighted to have solved and settled the enigma of Jim, especially so at the turn things had taken.

"You really were good, love, you've been hiding your light!"

"I'm always polishing my act. You were naughty, spying on me like you did. I was going to surprise you."

"You did that alright."

Peter patted my arm.

"I think I'll be off," he mouthed, carefully donning his jacket.

Max looked up.

"Take that off, take it off, party pooper. We're celebrating."

Peter coughed, smiling, and did as Max told him. So did I, which was to order champagne.

Max raised his fluted glass.

"To Lola Lamour, diva divine!"

"And all who sail in her," added Lola.

The bottle was not smashed, but the imbibers of its contents…

I woke with the feeling that someone had rearranged my room while I slept.

There was a faded poster on the wall, Cary Grant and Randolph Scott clowning by the pool. Not showbiz enough for Jim.

I sat up, shivering. My clothes were in a heap at the foot of the bed, and I was reaching for my shirt when there was a light knock on the door. The benign figure of Peter carrying a tray brought enlightenment.

The rush of champagne drank too fast. Calling cabs outside the 'Performing Ferret.' Vague journey. Spare room.

"Since you see fit not to join us, I thought I'd bring you yours in bed," said Peter, laughing. "How about coffee and croissants?"

"I don't think I could do croissants," I said, grabbing at the coffee. "Any chance of refreshing my memory about last night, the last part anyway?"

"Oh dear, like that is it? Well, though I do pride myself on my excellent Irish coffee, I do make it *rather* strong and fairly plentiful."

"And I drank fairly plentifully?"

"You were no stranger to the beaker. You know, you're quite sweet when you're inebriated. Up to a point. Max and Jim got you upstairs and tucked you in. Very efficient, I thought."

"Thorough," I added.

"Max said he was experienced."

Though it hurt to do it, I made a mental note to discuss this with Max later.

"My ablutions call," said Peter, breezing off to the bathroom.

Drinking coffee, I sat looking at the yellow crescent of pastry on its plate. It seemed to smile at me, slightly mocking.

Downstairs, Jim and Max greeted me with jocularly abusive remarks.

"Here's the boy wonder! Want something in that coffee? Hope you found your underwear!"

Actually, it was mostly Max. Jim, though sometimes swayed by Max, was usually kinder.

"Leave him alone," he said. "He's only little."

"Oh, I don't know, I've seen worse."

"I'm sure you have."

"What do you mean?"

"Nothing. If the cap fits…"

"There you are, you're having a dig."

This was my cue to leave. A Max and Jim spat was best avoided, and I felt a bit sorry for Peter as I went.

Walking home I was tempted to go into the Hope, though not because I wanted a drink. Peter's coffee nightcaps were still Irish dancing on my frontal lobes. Best to eschew the brew.

I hadn't seen Jayne since the day I left her cradling Declan. I didn't know if they had gone away again, or were going on as usual. I didn't know what usual was.

I went straight to the squat.

There was a letter giving me a start date for the job at the hospital and another card from Joo-lee. The latter raised my spirits when I noticed it had a British stamp on it. I couldn't read the post-mark, but it felt good to think of her near. Her message was not particularly enlightening:

'der billy, sweatheart, hope u r groovy and miss u. Won't be long now and u n I will be reunited, love, look out, look up, incoming! Jxxx.'

There was an imprinted lipstick kiss over the text, which smelled cosmetic and was smeared.

I woke later almost as confused as I had been that morning, flat out on the living room mattress like strewn laundry. It was seven thirty P.M. and the room was growing dark.

I got up, shivering, flicked the light switch. Nothing. The coin needed putting through the meter a few times. I remembered Max hinting to me about it for the last few days, 'I put it through *loads* of times, but it won't last forever if someone doesn't soon take *their* turn!'

I shuffled to the meter, feeling above the dials for the eternal token. It had gone. I searched my pockets for the necessary replacement. Nothing suitable.

Maybe Max had left some change lying around. After checking the kitchen, I went into his room, moving quietly even though I knew he wasn't there.

His bedside cupboard was bare. I sat in the dark on the bed, checking desperately along the underside of the mattress. Coins were reputed to get into all sorts of unlikely places, but not in this squat.

However, my forage was not fruitless. A small, leather bound notebook dropped to the floor. I retrieved the volume and took it over to the window, scrutinising the cover. Blank. But on the first page was an inscription, in Max's handwriting.

'Doctor Max's (nut) Casebook.'

The only place I could get change now was a pub. That would mean buying a drink. I slipped the book in my pocket.

The Blacksmiths Arms embraced very few customers that evening. Beneath a long, framed map of the Thames, I sat down just where it flowed out by Canvey Island and merged with the Medway at Sheerness.

Next to my untouched pint of Fullers ESB, I carefully placed Max's notebook, and sat looking at the grainy cover.

Maybe I ought to just return it…

I took a sip of the rich, malty beer.

It's not as though it were a diary, though.

A box, discarded in an ashtray, bore the inscription 'Blake's Impregnated Safety Matches.' Lying next to it were the stubby remains of a fat cigar, and a Quaver.

I decided to open the book the moment my beer reached the half-pint line.

The landlord came over to empty the ashtray, wiping it with an old cloth and replacing it on the table, before resuming his conversation with a man hunched smoking at the bar.

"So what happened down East Lane?"

"What?"

"The market, you was telling something about the market."

"Oh yeah. My mate Duggie, it's his first morning, right? So we gets there, still fucking dark, and he says, 'you set up the stall and I'll park the van.' I say to him, 'you can't drive!' Know what he says?"

"What?"

"I can go in a straight line!"

"What happened, he crash it?"

"Nah. He was all right as it happens."

"Have you seen Woolworth's?"

"Not much. I only pass it every fucking day."

"No, the back, they've only set fire to the back of it!"

"Who have?"

"Who do you think?"

Half-pint.

The first page of Max's book began, 'Martin Caulfield was sectioned because he was judged to be dangerously delusional. Why? Repeatedly shouting Tutankhamen at a bus driver. Turned out it was actually Tooting Common. No need to shout though. He thinks I'm sent to him by the Devil to tempt him to Hell.'

No harm there. Not like a real case file or something.

I flicked forward a few pages, and almost skipped a section headed 'Ms J Rothman', until I caught sight of the name 'July' further down the page.

The second half of my pint was accompanied by these words,

'Alcohol dependency, query other drugs. Thinks daughter of influential American tycoon. Tendency to paranoia, which she counters with incoherent revenge fantasies. July very flirtatious…'

I finished my beer and quickly scratched together enough for another. The electricity could wait.

'Has made passes at Martin, who calls her the Wife of Chaos, (wonder what *Mister* Chaos is like!), and I think is interested in me. Won't see psychiatrist but always accepts moi! Said other day she was Jane Solanas reincarnate, but she would spare me when the time came. Solanas invented the society for cutting up men, or SCUM. Hilarious. (note, find out if Solanas dead.) Must admit she has charm and is possibly rather smart…'

I was prevented, for the moment, from further reading by the arrival of Joe. He sat down opposite me.

"Hi, Billy, not interrupting I hope?"

"Nothing that can't wait. How's Mat…Alison?"

"No idea and don't care," he replied, stripping foil from the neck of his bottle of lager. "How's your Uncle Mike?"

"Eh? Oh, he's alright, I suppose, considering."

He drank his lager fast and offered to fetch us a round.

"I owe you one, Billy, you did me a favour the other week."

"I didn't really do anything."

"Yeah, man, it's like, you were the catalyst, putting Maitresse's hackles up, and spurring me to retaliate for once."

"She sounded pretty mad."

"So what? Maybe she is mad. Anyway, getting away from her was the best thing I could have done, only I just hadn't realised it. Cheers!"

"You haven't been seeing her then?"

"Nor anyone else. I'm like the Pope, or Morrisey, you know, celibate. How about you?"

"I don't know really."

"Free and easy!"

Disengaged and simple.

"I better get back," I said, "I'd invite you for a beer but I haven't got any and the meter's run out."

"If that's not your way of saying you don't really want to invite me, I've got some change and I could stretch to a few take-outs."

When we arrived at the squat, there was music playing and the lights were back on. Max, Jim and Peter were there, rekindling the party spirit. Max had draped a red something or other over a lamp, making the room look like a Chinese restaurant, and smell of singed silk.

"Hello boys!" he exclaimed, automatically sloshing vodka into cups and handing them our way.

Joe hung back in the doorway.

"None of us bites," said Peter, rising politely "At least I don't, can't really speak for these two."

Joe smiled and put down the bottles of beer he was clutching.

"*Love* the face furniture!" said Max, causing Joe to blush and fumble with one of his multiply pierced earlobes.

"Don't embarrass him," said Jim. "Here, come and have a seat."

"A place on the mattress actually," said Peter. "Which reminds me, did I tell you about this office temp who we nicknamed…"

"I think you did," I interrupted.

"Oh God, repeating myself, old age. I think I need another rocket fuel!"

"I don't think *I've* heard it," mused Max, pouring the requested shot.

Max's notebook was burning my pocket, so I mumbled something about the loo and hastened to his room, quietly sneaking the volume under the mattress, (that word again), and flushing the toilet on my way back. I knew I would probably seek to borrow that book again.

When I re-joined the others, I found Joe choking and laughing, Peter whacking him on the back.

"We've had the Maitresse story," explained Max.

"I wish I'd have thought of it," said Joe, recovering a little.

"I don't really get it," remarked Jim.

"Don't worry, dear, you just stick to what you're good at," said Max.

"My art," said Jim, fanning himself with fluttering fingers.

"That too, love," replied Max.

Innuendo and out the other.

Responsibility Sits Hard

Sunday afternoon, Max and Jim asleep, Peter and Joe departed, I switched on the television to watch 'Carry On Constable', and, just as Charles Hawtrey made his entrance with a caged budgie, there was a repeated knock at the door.

Jayne stood twiddling her hair, standing on her left foot with her right.

"Are you ok?" she asked quietly.

"Why not?" I answered.

"I don't know really. I've missed you, can I come in?"

I had a pan on the stove boiling water for tea. I rinsed out the teapot.

"How's Declan?"

"Alright, you know, same really."

I warmed the pot.

"He's asked me to marry him."

I poured boiling water on the leaves.

"You should get tea bags," she said, "it's awful messy that way."

"I prefer it."

"Have you got anything to say?"

"About tea?"

She smiled, but there were tears in her eyes. Or perhaps it was the steam.

"What did you say?" I asked, concentrating on the pot as I stirred the brew.

"I said I'd…"

"Think about it?"

She looked at her feet.

"Yeah."

We went into the living room. The film had got to the part where the new recruits rush naked from a cold shower.

"Leslie Phillips has quite a nice bum," said Jayne.

We watched for a while, sipping our tea in silence while Sid James's Sergeant berated the constables.

"It's ages since you were in the Hope," remarked Jayne.

I didn't answer.

"If I do consent, he wants me to go t' Ireland with him."

Consent. It sounded sad and old-fashioned, the way she said it with her soft accent.

"Ah, peat fires and pints of stout!" I said, unkindly.

"I don't know if I'm going yet," she replied.

"Only you can work that one out."

"I suppose."

"Well, let me know, won't you?"

"Are you closing the subject?"

"Only you can do that."

"Of course I'll let you know Billy."

Kenneth Williams was dragged along by a dog that collided with a scooter-riding Hawtrey.

"They're never as funny as you thought they were," commented Jayne, finishing her tea.

Neither of us was laughing.

"I got a job," I said.

"Christ, Billy, a foot on the rung."

"Of the scaffold."

"Gallows humour."

"I told you I was a swinger."

She kissed me on my neck.

"I'll see you."

Tease

I saw Liz was coming to Great Britain to play a 'selected' gig. This reminded me, among other things, that I had not played with the Floating Adults since our ambulance station thrash. High time *we* selected ourselves another venue. Mind you, we'd have to get back in touch with one another first.

Naturally I wanted to attend the Liz fest almost as much as I wanted to stay away.

The title of her new release, 'England Laid Me', piqued my curiosity.

Yet I knew I would only attend if the mood suddenly struck me, and would then probably be too late to get a ticket.

I wished all of this didn't bother me.

Max could see that it did, and was naturally delighted.

"I heard her on the radio," he chimed, "have you heard it?"

"I haven't got a radio."

"Let me think, 'North and South, to and fro, England laid me, laid me low'," he sang. " 'Bade me baby, made me go', something like that!"

His was never an arse from which the sun readily shone.

But I borrowed his radio one day, when there was nobody around, and I kept an ear out until I heard the song. It was never played. I doubt if Max had really heard it either. In fact it was he, I remembered, who had first told me about it. He probably invented the title.

Errant boys

Somebody was hammering at the door, causing the glass to rattle. I went downstairs and peered cautiously through the kitchen window, then went and opened.

"Declan, what are you playing at? It's about seven a.m. I thought you were…"

"It's ten thirty. Now, listen, I'm not one to call in favours, but I need your help, and I did fix your leccy. Also, if you *don't* assist me, I'm going to lock you in a room with a video machine playing endless Norman Wisdom films."

"You haven't got such a video. Or a player, for that matter."

"Can you be sure of that?"

"Well…"

"Mr. Grims*dale!*"

"Alright, alright, what do I have to do?"

"Nothing. I'm driving a car up North for someone, and I can't stand to drive alone."

"That's it?"

"Well, you could throw in a bit of map reading. This mate of mine is arriving in Liverpool, and he doesn't want to have to travel to London to collect his vehicle."

"Why's the car down here, and he's up there?"

"His family are mostly there, only his brother was down here, until he died, at which point my mate inherited the motor. He's over for the vehicle and the funeral as well, taking place in Liverpool. Which reminds me."

"Of what?"

"Doesn't matter. Look, come on, we're on a schedule."

"Now?"

"Well, I could ask them to postpone the funeral."

"Why would they have to do that?"

He scratched his cheek.

"Well, the car's needed for the occasion."

The car had been left parked outside the brother's semi-detached in Finchley, and Declan and I were walking a street named 'Crooked Usage' trying to spot it.

"I think I see it," said Declan, stopping.

"Let's get it then. You have the keys I suppose?"

"To the house, yes. The car keys are inside."

"So come on, you're the one who said we're on a schedule."

"Yeah. Ok."

But he seemed reluctant to hurry.

"Listen, Billy, there's something about this little job."

"Yes?"

"Yeah. It's like they said, since I'm taking the car, it makes sense if I take the brother along too. Sort of kill two birds with one stone."

I sat on a low wall.

"*Take him along?* What's the car, a fucking hearse?"

"Not exactly. More of a Nissan Sunny."

"And was the brother a big man?"

"How should I know? Will you stop asking so many daft questions? Look, there's the place."

Declan pulled a set of keys from his pocket and selected the Yale.

I stopped.

"Are you telling me he's in there alone?"

"I shouldn't think he's been feeling much like company. Besides, there's no body down here to sit with him. His mother's too ill to travel. He died sort of suddenly."

"How?"

"He just kinda stopped living. Will you come on?"

I followed him through the hall and into the front room. There were photographs of children on the mantelpiece, and several pornographic videos scattered about the carpet. The coffin was supported on four kitchen chairs, the lid propped up beside it against the fireplace.

"This is not possible," I said quietly.

"The car's got a roof rack," whispered Declan.

"That's not exactly what I meant."

There was a sudden shriek.

"Christ almighty!" exclaimed Declan, "I forgot about the fucking parrot."

The bird regarded us, head swaying, with mischievously beady eyes.

"Please tell me that's not coming with us as well," I muttered, for some reason trying to prevent the creature from hearing.

"No way," Declan assured me. He tipped some seed into the cage and checked the water.

"Nice one!" screeched Polly.

Declan peered into the box. He shook his head.

"Dear me, he doesn't look well. Suicide. His wife left with the kids. Do you want to see him before I fix the lid?"

I didn't move.

"Ok!"

I watched him secure the coffin.

"How far do you think we're going to get with that thing on the roof?"

Declan paused.

"You've a point there. We'll have to put a sheet over it, disguise it a bit. Here, catch!"

He threw over a coil of rope.

"That's what he used to hang himself!"

I failed to catch.

"Only kidding. He took pills."

I went upstairs to get a sheet and returned to find Declan stacking videos on the coffin. He grinned.

"This is great! This'll disguise the shape, and when the job's done I can sell the tapes. Quids in."

Once trussed up, I had to admit that the load might have been any old luggage, but I was still not relishing the trip. Declan, however, seemed to be starting to enjoy it.

"Come on, Billy, cheer up will you? You're not the one in the box. Grab a hold."

We made unlikely pallbearers struggling out with our burden, me swearing and Declan laughing.

"Mind the paintwork, Billy, steady, steady. Wind's getting up, we'll have to lash him down well."

He punched my arm,

"Hey ho, let's go!"

As soon as we hit the motorway, Declan chucked the makings of a joint onto the map I was straining to read.

"Skin up," he cheerfully ordered.

"You know I'm useless at it. We'll end up with a drainpipe."

He sighed.

"What *would* I do without you?"

He snatched back the gear and, positioning his wrists at the top of the wheel, proceeded to fiddle with papers.

"You can at least manage to sort out the shit I suppose?"

He kicked the cassette player, which started blasting Motorhead.

I lit a match and softened the resin, shoe polish and cardamom waft, and crumbled some onto the long collage of papers he had somehow managed to collate.

"You can manage the tobacco I suppose?" he yelled, putting his foot down and shearing into the fast lane without indicating. I sprinkled some in from a split cigarette, and Declan took over to roll it. He was an expert, neat and tight, but it didn't help his steering.

He sucked down a long, deep draw.

"You're a hard man," he observed, exhaling, "making me roll joints while driving, and me lacking in the full Monty finger-wise. '*The ace of spades, the ace of spades*', turn it up will you?"

I could hear the coffin reverberating overhead, and thought of the brother lying cold in the dark, his own porn collection rattling above his body. Rain lashed the windscreen, and the wipers were slow.

"Yes, come on!" shouted Declan, as something by Black Sabbath wailed out.

"Is this your tape?" I asked.

"Personal best!" he bellowed.

The wind got so strong that Declan had to compensate with the steering.

"Fucking never say die!" he cackled.

Through the deluged rear window I noticed the driver of the car behind was flashing his lights, just as one of the videos was whipped clear of the sheet, and sent flying straight at his windscreen. As it clung there, held by the force of the wind, a blue light began to oscillate on the roof of the vehicle, to the accompaniment of a wailing siren.

Declan trundled us onto the hard shoulder and switched off the music.

Two officers approached, and one started prodding the load on the roof. The other strolled slowly over to Declan's lowered window.

He peered in at us, then scrutinised the cover of the video he had retrieved from the front of his patrol car.

"Fisting Lolitas," he said dryly.

"The wind's got up," answered Declan.

"I dare say. Do you realize you're shedding your load?"

The other cop was tugging at the sheet.

"Thanks, officer," murmured Declan.

"Don't mention it."

He tapped the video box with a stubby finger.

"Any more of this sort of material on board?"

Declan smiled, and as he stalled, I let the roach and the rizlas fly free from my window. Declan had swallowed the remainder of the dope as soon as he realised we had company.

"Take a look at this," came a shout from the rear. "They've only got a bloody coffin up here!"

The first officer exhaled sharply through his teeth.

"Oh dear me! You wouldn't have a lot more of this filth stashed inside I suppose?"

"Oh no, no more videos," replied Declan. "It's actually, well, more of a…"

"Corpse?"

We nodded.

They searched us both, breathalysed Declan, and there followed a period of questioning, with a lot of checking up on radios. The main focus of interest appeared to be the porn stash, which, as the actual owner was beyond the law, they simply decided to confiscate. Once the officers had finished loading the tapes into the boot of their car, one of them came over and helped us tie the sheet more securely around the coffin.

"This is highly irregular," he said, "though apparently, since you possess the requisite paperwork, certificate of death, et cetera, not actually illegal. Therefore, I'm prepared to let you go. Behave yourselves."

"Thanks," I said.

He tapped the side of the coffin.

"Yes, well you'd better be on your way. Don't want him to be late for his own funeral, do we?"

He strolled away with the air of a man about to re-tell his joke.

Declan drove steadily away, a smile beginning to spread across his face as he started to realise the effects of his Lebanese lunch. The police followed us for a while, and when they turned off, Declan swerved out of the slow lane, and settled for middle.

We droned on for several miles, until, on sudden impulse, Declan veered off into a services, to the angry sound of honking horns.

"Lighten the fuck up," he shouted, laughing. "In a few years you'll be like your man on the roof."

We had a piss and a coffee. Declan also consumed the greasiest fried egg in the world, some pale orange beans and a reddish shrivelled sausage.

"I have to watch the old blood sugar," he explained.

While he scoffed, I studied the map, straining to realise the route to Birkenhead.

Declan prodded my arm with a fork,

"We can stop one night at the mothers', but we'll have to doss on the floor as my mate's having the spare room. Then, I get paid, a little something for you, and home we hitch."

He licked a shred of egg white from his lower lip, burped twice, wiped his mouth with the back of his hand and stood up.

"Easy money!"

I didn't sleep particularly well at Mrs Ryan's. Perhaps it was the unique tone of Declan's snoring, the unwanted attention of a West Highland terrier, the insistence on the part of a carriage clock of chiming the quarter hour, or maybe just the shadowy presence in the room of a coffin draped with a table cloth.

Declan, however, was no stranger to slumber, and woke early, yawning through unbrushed teeth.

"That dog's really taken to you," he observed, wandering over to the window in his underpants. The animal concerned had somehow forced most of itself into my sleeping bag, and was trying to lick my face.

"At least he hasn't got your breath," I replied.

"How you come up with these witty rejoinders I will never know."

He bent down close to the coffin.

"Rise and shine!" he shouted, rapping his knuckles on the lid.

Mrs Ryan came in with some tea, and Declan lingered shyly behind the box, arms crossed over his flat chest.

"Top of the morning Mrs R," he said, nodding.

"Thanks lads," she said, pouring the brew. "I don't know how I'd have managed it without you. Are you sure you can't stop for the funeral?"

"Ah, no," answered Declan. "You see, Billy here, he's a busy man, a lot of appointments and such."

"Sure, I understand, is it a civil servant you are?"

"Not really…"

"He's a doctor, consultant, you know, waiting list as long as your arm," interjected Declan, pulling on his jumper.

Mrs Ryan looked concerned.

"I hope I've not put you out too much?"

Declan put his arm around her shoulders.

"Don't trouble yourself, Mrs R. Billy wanted to help at a time like this. It's in his nature. Is there any toast going?"

Declan's mate came down at about ten and went straight into the kitchen mumbling about aspirins. Declan followed him, there was a brief murmur of conversation, and we were off.

Getting back to London took nearly nine hours. The first two we spent being showered with spray from the relentless stream of passing traffic. Our piece of cardboard with 'SOUTH' scribbled on it in biro was not proving effective. But that first lift finally arrived, an articulated lorry, grinding and hissing, the driver beckoning.

We sat up in the cab, and the owner told us about his vehicle, establishing from the start that it was to be an 'I talk, you listen' sort of ride. The vehicle was new, and he spoke of it like one house-proud, drawing our attention to the neat sleeping area behind our seat, a small mattress and duvet, matching pillowcase, "all in brushed nylon".

I noticed a mini-sized plastic dustpan and brush at my feet, and a packet of wet wipes on the dash. Unfortunately it was a short lift, and we were soon standing in the drizzle at a services.

We were trying to ignore the taunts of passing drivers, when some young blokes in a Peugeot pulled over. They waited to see the dawning hope on our faces, a couple of hesitant paces, before starting to drive away. Declan remained impassive, waited for the car-full of derisive laughter to rejoin the motorway, then spun a pebble concealed in his hand with such force and accuracy that their rear windscreen shattered.

"No U-turns on the motorway," he uttered with a smile.

"Maybe so," I replied, pointing, "but pulling over onto the hard shoulder is allowed."

The driver of the damaged car was already walking back towards us, followed by a couple of the other passengers.

"You're only supposed to do that in an emergency," observed Declan.

"Maybe they consider this to be one."

"I think it fucking might be."

Our attention was so fixed on the approaching posse that it was not until the owner spoke that we noticed the Jaguar XJ6 that had drawn up beside us.

"You guys want a ride?"

As the powerful engine bore us to safety, the driver introduced himself. He was called David, a Canadian with oiled, brushed back hair, and a cashmere cardigan.

"Say," he remarked, as we passed the afflicted motorcar. "Looks like they've had a little trouble! Do you guys think there's anything we can do to assist?"

We shook our heads quite a lot.

"I guess not," he said, and continued driving, foot reassuringly down.

He was chatty, urbane. Addressing us, he always took care to use our names.

"So, Declan, where're you headed exactly? You ok in the back there, Billy? Music not too loud? Would I be, like, totally out of order if I asked you about your hands, Declan? I mean, were you in some sort of accident?"

Declan laughed loudly,

"David, I am some sort of accident."

"You crazy Irish, I love it. I have just got to visit your country."

"Well, when I'm married, and thing's settle down, you'll have to come and see us."

"Well, watch out I might just hold you to that. Getting married, huh? Tell me about the lucky girl."

I concentrated on the music.

For the next few days, I wandered, wondering, trying to get my nose in gear for a spell at the grindstone.

The tiresome cycle of dole/broke/dole/broke was breaking me up, but the thought of the alternative didn't cheer me.

Then the eve of my starting date arrived.

So did Joo-Lee.

She was all tanned and lean, number one haircut and her braces off.

"Hey Billy-o!" she said, grabbing my shoulders and giving me a shake.

Max peered round his door.

"Oh, hello dear, all right?" he said, receding.

She looked at his closed door for some seconds, as if struggling with a memory, and suddenly laughed.

"Look at you, Billy," she said. "Still crazy after all these beers!"

"Are you suggesting a drink?"

"I'm off it, Billy, I've cleaned up my act. All's I drink these days is Asti Spumante. No more spirits coming back to haunt me, no more cider inside her!"

"I'm all out of Asti, I'm afraid."

"Well, let's have tea, and you can tell me what you've been up to."

Max reappeared, fastening his tie.

"I have to go," he said. "Nice to see you back, July."

Joo-Lee frowned at him, pointing with an index finger that slowly uncoiled from her fist, then clapped her palms, lowered her arms to her sides, smiled, and turned away.

"Well, toodle-pip," said Max.

I poured tea, and Joo-Lee sipped quietly. She took a strip of tablets from her shoulder bag.

"I have to take these for a while. They said I could only get out if I was com*pliant*. She popped one.

"Are you staying over?" I asked.

"Actually, that was something I was gonna ask, only I lost my flat, and my dad doesn't want me in England so he won't help out, so I was wondering…"

I nodded, and she gave me her biggest smile.

"Don't go anywhere, I'm gonna forage for Spumante!" she exclaimed.

She paused in the doorway.

"That guy, he works at the booby hatch, right?"

"Right."

She slammed the door.

I went into Max's room and felt under the mattress. There was a magazine entitled 'Members Only', but no notebook. I guessed Max must have taken it to work.

Joo-Lee returned with three bottles of fizzy wine.

"Daddy still sends money, but never enough to afford to rent."

She fired a cork across the room, which ricoched off the wall and hit Vic's cat on the back of the head.

"Sorry Pussy!" laughed Joo-Lee.

The animal walked stiffly out of the room, shuddering with indignation.

"Hey, I wrote some stuff," said Joo-Lee, "you wanna hear some?"

"Sure," I replied, though I wasn't.

"This is called 'Catharsis'," she announced, unfolding a page of lined paper on which she had written in pencil.

"Morning," she read, "birds fall, flailing, feathers loose. Bed falls apart in angry pain. Hanging curtains of the intrigue of death. The glazed smile of the white-coat man. Skin, bone, feathers and fur. They swarm over the sheets. The night was a dark gunge. Day is a white feather."

She swallowed wine.

"Silly, huh?"

"I wouldn't say that."

"You're nice."

She moved closer, resting her head on my shoulder. The smell of Paco Rabanne, but no cigarette smoke.

"I gave up," she whispered.

I poured the last of the bottle, as she twisted the cork on the next.

"Do you find it hard to be positive?" she asked.

"What about?"

"Oh, you know, just generally. I do. A girlfriend told me to think of a really, like, affirmative statement, and to write it out hundreds of times."

"Did you?"

"Well, I had this really neat sentence, 'things *will* go my way', and so I got a big pad of paper and started writing."

"Did it help?"

"I dunno, the pen ran out."

She sipped some wine and shook her head around like a boxer limbering up.

"Oh. I start work tomorrow," I said.

"Great! I'll be here with your dinner when you come home."

Knuckle Down

I woke with a wine head and acid stomach, scrambling to the bathroom and gulping water from the tap. Six A.M. No point in trying for more sleep. I was due to report for work at eight.

I nicked some of Max's ground coffee, brewing up a soupy one, and looked at the letter from the hospital to check the details. Incredibly I must originally have misread it, for the starting time for the rest of the week was eight, but on my first day I was not expected until two o'clock in the afternoon.

I climbed back into bed beside a snoring Joo-Lee, and lay staring at the ceiling as the caffeine started to tweak at my brain. I felt irritated at myself for letting Joo-Lee draw me into a wine binge, but mainly for not having concentrated when reading that letter. I could have blissfully slept late and reported for work fresh and alert in the afternoon.

Instead I was gratingly conscious and unrelaxed. While Joo-Lee slept on obliviously, the routines of hospital portering started running round my brain.

The chimes of a Mister Softee van distortedly rending the air with 'Whistle while you work' had me bolt up and jump out from the covers.

Must have dropped off.

There was barely enough time left for me to get to work, never mind the whistling.

Declan had given me his bike a few weeks back, having perfected travel card forgery with razor blade and glue. It was the only way I could make it on time, so I carried the two-wheeler down the stairwell, and wobbled off down Rotherhithe Street in the rain. Only a few minutes late, I chained the steed to some railings opposite the Throat Nose and Ear hospital, and looked up at the grey building.

A small plaque beneath the main title read, 'Institute of laryngology and otology.'

Running a finger around my shirt collar, I swallowed dryly as I entered.

"I'm William Bedford," I said to the woman at Reception.

She smiled at me.

"Are you visiting a patient?"

"I don't think so. I'm supposed to be starting as a porter."

She looked at a clipboard, and I got a sudden feeling it had all been a mistake. Perhaps I wanted it so.

But she nodded, handing me a visitor's book.

"That's right Mr Bedford, would you like to sign here and print your name? They'll sort you out with an I.D. badge later."

She directed me to a small office in which Mr Carter, the Head Porter, was expecting me. I knocked, and a muffled voice with an Australian twang bade me enter.

Mr Carter was a small, grey haired man in his mid-forties, tanned, with a beer belly. He extended a hairy-backed hand, and gripped mine firmly with short, faintly freckled fingers.

"Great to have you aboard, great stuff!" he said. "William, isn't it?"

He seemed to wink at me, but I was soon to learn that this was a facial tic, his left eyelid flickering and causing the corner of his lip to twitch as if it were attached with invisible twine.

"Have a coffee, Billy. Don't mind if I call you Billy, Billy?"

His name was Brian, and, as he sat with me, sipping instant, and running through 'the basics', I felt myself gradually relaxing.

"We're not a bad lot," he laughed, suddenly standing and flinging open the door.

"Hey, Austin!" he yelled. No response.

"Where's that bastard skiving off this time?" he mumbled, smiling at me with a double wink. He fumbled with a pager on his belt, and shortly afterwards Austin appeared.

He was about twenty, standing tall and skinny in the doorway, with a right eye that looked sideways towards his left. As he grinned into the office, displaying several gold caps on his teeth, it was difficult to tell which of us he was looking at.

"I was going to the morgue," he said.

"Pick up?"

"Yeah man."

"O.K. Won't keep you. Just wanted to introduce the new feller. Billy, Austin, Austin, Billy."

I stood up and we shook. Austin wore a lot of rings, and his palm was damp.

"Alright?" he asked.

He wore a light-blue short-sleeved smock and rubber shoes, garments, I realised, I too would soon be sporting.

"Why don't you take Billy with you, show him the fridge?" suggested Brian.

"Yeah man," said Austin, beckoning for me to follow.

He strode quickly down corridors, arms swinging at his sides in a sort of swaggering march. One forearm bore the tattoo of a lion wearing a crown, the site of which, judging by the scars, had either been injured, or an attempt made to remove the design.

"Here we are, my man," he said, gesturing with a flourish towards the double doors to the mortuary.

"Got to get out Mr Perkins, he's due to be picked up. Came in for surgery, cancer of the nose, died before the knife even touch him. Nice geezer too."

Inside were neat rows of steel doors, each closed on an oblong fridge. Austin grabbed a handle and hauled out Mr Perkins, who lay under a light cotton sheet.

"When they finally put you to bed, noone tucks you in," laughed Austin. "You want to say hello?"

He tweaked the corner of the sheet.

I shook my head, although, in a way, of course, I did feel curious to see what the old man looked like, presuming for that matter that he was old.

I smiled thinly.

"He ain't offended," said Austin.

I helped him to manoeuvre Mr Perkins down to the back exit.

"If you're ever admitted here," grinned Austin, "better pray you go out the same way you came in."

A hearse was parked outside, chrome gleaming in the pale afternoon sunshine, droplets of rain on its polished black bonnet.

We wheeled over its next passenger.

My first day passed unexpectedly quickly, and the work didn't look too daunting. Austin seemed to spend quite a lot of time smoking on the stairs, and I had a couple with him to be sociable. Brian appeared to be a genial boss.

"Roll on Thursday!" he remarked, as we knocked off for the day.

"Thursday?" I said.

Brian and Austin exchanged a smile.

"Round the corner, 'Prince of Wales', opening time," said Brian, "It's a sort of unwritten rule, eh Austin?"

"Every Thursday, man," confirmed Austin.

"Makes the weekend come faster," added Brian.

I wondered what they were like on an early Friday shift.

"Last one in buys the first round!" shouted Brian through the window of his car. "Drop you off anywhere?"

"No thanks, I've got my bike," I yelled.

He drove off, and I noticed Austin grinning out of the passenger window.

The Prince of Wales. At least I would have somewhere other than The Hope. Also, the Scala cinema was round the corner, although the thought of it reminded me of going there with Jayne.

I walked over to the railings where I had chained my bike, but it wasn't there. Thinking I might have made a mistake about the location, I glanced up and down the road, but there was nothing attached to the railings apart from a small laminated sign. 'Bicycles chained to these railings will be removed.'

Imitation of Wife

'Winter is here and it's going on two years,' announced the voice of Joey Ramone on the jukebox. I swallowed my London Pride and stared at the frost on the window of the Blacksmiths' Arms. It seemed like ages since I had been to the Hope. For all I knew Jayne and Declan could have been long gone to old Erin.

Having walked home from work, I had now drunk the last of my money. I went to the squat, and Joo-Lee was sitting cross-legged outside the door.

"Didn't I give you a key?" I asked.

"Yeah I lost it. Open up Billy I'm dying of exposure."

"You should get some proper shoes," I said, eyeing her battered flip-flops.

"I can't wear 'em, I got claustrophobic feet," she explained.

"In that case," I said, as we went in, "I think mine must be agoraphobic."

"Fear of agro and wide open faces," said Joo-Lee, as much to herself as anything.

I started making tea, and she asked,

"When do you get a holiday?"

"I've just started. You have to apply for annual leave."

"*One* has to apply," she corrected. "Jesus, sounds like the army! Would you get shot if you went a.w.o.l?"

"They might get shot of me."

"Drag! I wanted to take you to Paris. I got some money from Dad."

"I thought you were persona non grate."

"Spare me your fantasies, Billy. I told him I got married."

"Who to?"

"To *whom*. To you, silly!"

"And he thinks its hunky dory to find you're suddenly married to someone he's never met, never mind not being invited to the wedding?"

"Sure! I sent him your photo, and he hates ceremonies. And England."

"The two tend to go hand in hand. And I'm English, remember."

"I told him you were Irish, it's cool. So, get some animal leave and we can go on honeymoon, *lune de miele*, *a Paris, grace a Papa*."

I noticed there was a pan of water on the stove, for pasta, but the gas had not been lit.

"Oh, yeah, sorry. I was gonna cook for ya, like, come home and your dinner's on the table, dutiful wife waiting with pipe and slippers, not hers, obviously, only the gas ran out, and so did I."

I picked up an opened can of tomatoes.

Joo-Lee took it from me.

"There, you see? I started."

She fumbled among some cans on the shelf.

"It's just, I'm not really… Come on, come on, I know you're there!"

She smiled, lifting down a cup from which she drank the remaining wine.

"Bottoms up, derrieres in the air," she said, swinging open the fridge door to reveal several bottles. She added another from her bag.

"I love this icebox 'cause it always has space for booze!"

"Only because it never contains anything else."

I watched her draw the cork from a fresh bottle.

"What the hell else d'ya need?"

She poured for us both.

"So, Daddy came through, eh?"

"Uh hu." She poured, and took a sip. "Wine comes in at the mouth, and love at the eye, and that's all you need and all you know," she intoned. "That's Keats. Or Yeats, maybe."

"Are you supposed to drink with your medication?"

"Or maybe it was Wordsworth. Oh yeah, I have to, otherwise the pills would get stuck in my oesophagus, dissolving there and eating through the tissue, before finally melting into my lungs and causing an agonising death."

"Not an ideal scenario."

"Exact-a-mundo." She passed me a cup. "Cheers, dear! Oh, I meant to say, I'm planning on having a baby."

I swallowed.

"Planning?"

"Yeah, get this, we send Daddy some photos of me with, like, a pillow or something up my jumper, and get someone to give me a few shots of their kid for Grandpa!"

"And Grandma?"

"You know we don't mention her."

"You don't think Pop will want to meet the little one?"

"That's the joy of it, he'd rather send money. He's not big on little kids. He's not really big on anyone. His life is a sort of facsimile. Kinda like, Zerox man."

"Well, it's your scam."

"Hark at the supportive husband! You're supposed to be over the moon."

"Howling at it, more like."

"Grrr!"

Ours' was no ordinary sham marriage.

Soft Focus

"I got a new camera," said Austin, as we stood waiting for the lift.

"Do you take a lot of pictures?"

"Yeah, man, that's why I needed to get this really professional camera, SLR, loads of features. I'm sort of semi-professional."

"What, like functions?"

"Yeah, I done McCartney, Rod Stewart…"

He trailed off nonchalantly as we entered the lift. There was a mirror inside, in which I glanced at him as he tweaked his hair with a wide-toothed comb.

"I'm doing some glamour stuff soon," he continued, looking perfectly serious. "Erotic material. I'll tell you something…"

He fell silent as a consultant with a group of students joined us at level two, and the subject didn't come up again once we were busy.

It was Thursday, so I was prepared for my initiation drink-up in the Prince of Wales. Joo-Lee had subbed me a brown drinking voucher, so I could hold my own with the rounds.

We met Brian in the changing room. He was applying roll-on under his arms, and whistling the theme from 'Black Orpheus.'

"Hello girls," he said, tossing the roll-on to Austin. He sniffed it, wrinkling his nose.

"That smells disgusting you know. What the ladies like is the natural smell of a man."

He closed his eyes and smelled himself from bicep to shoulder.

"Aint that right, Billy boy?"

"Depends what the man smells like I suppose."

This seemed to amuse Brian. He stopped combing his hair and bent forward, silently rocking and colouring puce, before inhaling a rasping gulp of air to be finally expelled as loud barking laughter.

"I like it, Billy!"

We were the first customers in the pub, greeted by the almost mournful pale face of the sandy haired barman, Bernard, as he opened up.

"Gentlemen," he said.

"Says who?" answered Brian, guffawing.

I paid for a Fosters for Brian, a Guinness for Austin, and a pint of Courage Best, and we sat on velour-upholstered stools at the bar.

After a long sup, consuming a third of his pint, Brian put his arm behind me, clapping me so firmly between the shoulders that I spilled beer.

"I think you're going to do fine, mate," he said, and quickly drained the rest of his lager and scattered notes on the bar for another round. I was soon to learn that he always kept his drinking money on the bar in front of him, never sat at a table, and rarely left until the money before him ran out.

Austin drank slowly, sometimes missing a drink when buying a round.

"I don't like to rush things," he said. "A good thing should be given time, that's what my old man used to say."

"And now he's doing time," said Brian.

"That aint funny."

"Sorry, mate, no offence. How's the photography coming along?"

"Yeah, you know, I was telling Billy, I've got some glamour work coming up. Erotic photos, for a magazine."

Brian nudged me with his elbow.

"One of those top shelf jobbies eh?" he said, lighting a menthol cigarette.

"Yeah, I'll have to hire a studio and that, you know."

I wondered how he got the assignments. As far as I knew he rarely left the flat where he lived with his Aunt. She did all the cooking and housework, while he put in some housekeeping money. I didn't like to question him, though Brian had no such compunction.

"You'll have to bring some of the pictures in," he said. "We wouldn't mind a look at the old nudie shots, eh Billy?"

I smiled, not committing myself. Austin stared at the shamrock that Bernard had expertly drawn on the head of his pint.

"You never did show me those Rod Stewart wedding snaps," said Brian, again using his elbow to gently prod me in the ribs.

"I told you, man, those were restricted, it was a special deal. I might let you see some of the nude work."

"Nothing too pervy I hope."

Austin looked like he wanted the subject dropped.

"Brian tells me you're in the Territorial Army," I remarked.

He drank a careful mouthful and slowly replaced his glass on a beer mat.

"I don't talk about it much."

Brian's winking tic flickered furiously and he got up and hurried off to the toilet.

"He's a funny geezer sometimes," observed Austin. "Anyway, a lot of T.A. stuff is secret, you know, can't be too careful. I will bring those photos in though. He don't think I will, but he's got another think coming."

"Cheer up, ladies," said Brian, returning.

He beckoned to Bernard, pointing at our glasses.

"Same again?" said Bernard.

Brian nodded, climbing with some effort onto his stool.

"This feller here, Billy," he said, putting his arm around Austin's shoulders, "can be a right moody bugger, can't you mate? A right Miles Davis."

"I hate jazz," said Austin, shrugging him off.

We had come in at five, and by seven I was already feeling heady. Austin seemed to slow down and withdraw into his beer, but Brian burned on it, his face reddening, voice growing louder. His conversation became increasingly, frankly personal, referring to his 'friend', with whom he shared a flat, and their long relationship. He also began to accompany his chat with frequent physical contact, clapping us on the back, and clasping our hands in both of his in a shake that almost had us off our stools.

"Back home," he told us, "the only blokes who carried an umbrella were poufs. Imagine what I felt like arriving in London as a young man and seeing all those fellas going over Waterloo Bridge! Jeeze, I thought I was in Heaven."

"If I had a quid for every time I've heard that," murmured Austin.

"I could make you a rich man," replied Brian.

"No thank you."

Undaunted by Austin's jaded demeanour, Brian continued to drink fast. He managed a few more funny anecdotes, before ascending to such a high of inebriation that he became incapable of coherent speech. Thereafter he resorted to clumsy sexual innuendo, suggesting several times that I should go home with him.

"You won't be disappointed," he slurred, pointing at his crotch. "It's a pole, a bloody pole, mate."

Austin was obviously accustomed to our boss's drinking spiral. He more or less ignored him, until, with a knowing air, he slipped down from his stool and calmly prevented Brian from falling off his.

"Usually happens," he said. "See you later."

He guided the almost sleeping Brian towards the exit.

Nine-thirty P.M.

My first Thursday session at the Prince of Wales was over.

Turkey Drummers

"How come you never play any gigs?" asked Joo-Lee one frozen, wasted afternoon.

"We don't even rehearse."

"'xactly! The Floating Adults have done floated down the pan. I never even heard you play."

"You haven't missed much."

"What made you start playing drums?"

"God made me. He needed a musician to accompany Gabriel."

She snorted.

"Boozician, more like! I reckon you just couldn't be bothered to learn a proper instrument."

"There's nothing improper about drums."

"See, classic avoidance tactic. You know I'm right."

Max hurried in and huddled near the gas fire, shuddering in a bathrobe.

"Christ it is sub fucking zero in my room. There's ice on the inside of the window. I swear my sheets are almost frozen."

"They're probably just crispy," I said.

He peered out from inside the towelling hood of his gown as if only just noticing me.

"Thank you, Billy, for your helpful suggestion. I suppose you'll be lounging by the fire all afternoon while I do good in the Community for the Confused?"

"And what do you propose he *should* he do on his day off?" asked Joo-Lee.

"In this world," said Max, "there are basking sharks, drifting through the sea with their mouths wide open to receive food, and lions, who stalk, chase, kill and drag to cover prey heavier than themselves. Which most resembles Billy?"

"What are you on?" asked Joo-Lee.

"It's about thrust, thrust! Who dares wins. Seize the day!"

"I'm getting some wine," sighed Joo-Lee. "I'm gonna stalk it, chase it and drag it back to my lair. Pity it won't be heavier than me though."

"I probably most resemble the things floating around that get sucked in by the shark," I murmured, wishing Max would let a little heat pass his crouching form.

He yawned and stretched.

"Well I at least try to emulate the lion."

"Really?" said Joo-Lee, "I thought you usually dragged your food back from Tescos in a cab."

She set down cups and bottle, nudging Max aside to get near the fire.

"And anyway it's the female lions that do all the hunting."

Max let out a low fart, unbroken for some three seconds, culminating in a high, rasping vibrato.

"Whatever."

He watched the wine pouring into cups.

"Oh, fuck it, I'm calling sick! Pour one for me while I go to the 'phone. Better still, I'll be mother while one of you goes for me. There's a fiver in it."

"You forget that my husband is gainfully employed, and I'm wastefully supported," said Joo-Lee.

"You bastards, I'm not dressed, it's like Siberia out there! Oh, please, I'll owe you!"

Encouraged by the thought, I got up.

"You just lie there basking, I'll made your excuses."

"Billy you're an angel, albeit a fallen one."

Winter had got a firm grip on us, cleaving in great stacks of stalactites under eaves, choking pipes and clinging to ledges. Massive icy waterfalls spewed from broken overflows, frozen static.

My feet were numb before I even got to the 'phone box, and I regretted agreeing to the trip. The going was precarious and I almost slipped several times, but the 'phone, at least, was working.

"I'm ringing for Max Subotsky, he won't be in, I'm afraid. Very bad diarrhoea."

I hurried back, stomping and shivering into the squat.

"Close the door," shouted Max. "That draught'll freeze my balls off."

"Please and thank you would be nice."

"Thank you, oh thank you!" He turned the gas up full and spread his toes nearer the heat. "What did you tell them, flu?"

"You'll see."

He eyed me shrewdly, trying to read my mind. Joo-Lee grinned, prodding me in the ribs.

"What?" said Max.

"Forget it," said Joo-Lee, leaning on him and lighting a cigarette.

"I suppose it's very beautiful out there?" he said. "Winter wonderland, fairy palaces?"

"Hairy phalluses!" sang Jim, emerging from the bathroom.

"I wondered when you'd surface."

"You make me sound like a whale! Funny that, in a way, 'cause I'm off for that audition now."

"What audition?"

"I swear you never listen to me. I told you, 'Divine', he's doing a video. I'm up for a chorus girl or something. Aren't you late for work?"

"Got my shifts mixed up."

"Oh well, toodle-oo!"

Max drank more wine, smiling fondly.

"I love Jim like I've never loved before," he told us.

"God, I'm goin' for a piss," remarked Joo-Lee.

"She is *so* unromantic," said Max, examining the spaces between his toes.

"Do you think she's, you know, ok?" I asked.

"I think time will tell, Billy. She seems..."

But he was interrupted by her return, kicking open the door, laughing.

"H-Yell-O, fuckers!" she exclaimed, and sank smiling and drooley onto Max's lap. They smooched, lips outpursed.

"She's a sweetie really, isn't she?" said Max.

"Yeah, I am actually. Look, I forgot " said she, ferreting a small object from her pocket. " I got you this."

"A toe ring!" beamed Max. "She cares!"

Joo-Lee spent several minutes trying to slot the silver trinket onto one of Max's nether digits, before rolling onto her back and giggling.

Max lit her a cigarette, put it in her mouth and slipped the ring onto the middle toe of his right foot.

"It's lovely darling," he said, squeezing her knee.

A windowpane suddenly cracked with a loud report that had us all temporarily transfixed. The freeze seemed to be taking control of the building. A chill razor edge of wind cut through the vertical crack in the glass, whittling our cheeks.

"Scary," remarked Max, fiddling with the silver band that now encircled his toe.

"I really love the winter," sighed Joo-Lee, overbalancing the bottle she was cradling, and baptizing her chest.

"Oopsy," she smiled. "You got any drugs Max?"

He narrowed his eyes.

"You're taking enough without my help."

"You can be so mean."

She pulled off her jumper and snuggled up to him, closer to the fire.

The air around me was growing steadily cooler. I tried to position myself in a gap between them, hoping to benefit from a little used heat.

"We need some music," suggested Joo-Lee. She clambered to the record player, scratching the needle abruptly into the opening synth-strains of 'Fade to Grey'.

"We do really, I suppose," said Max, after a few moments of desultory listening.

"Bad choice," said Joo-Lee, "Max's gone glazy. C'mon Billy, I'm taking you to the pub."

I swallowed bitter and stared again at the frost on the windows of the Blacksmiths Arms.

1.30 P.M. and it was nearly dark.

"Put another coin in the jukebox, baby," said Joo-Lee, toying with her glass of lemonade. Rotherhithe pubs were not big on Asti Spumante.

"I'm gettin' so bored, Billy."

"Thanks."

"Not with you, but, you know. Maybe I should have some cider."

"I don't suppose it makes any difference."

"What does that mean?"

"Well, if you are alright with wine, I don't suppose cider'll do you any harm."

"I'm tryin' real hard to keep straight remember?"

"I didn't say you weren't. Anyway wine's stronger than cider."

"So you're saying I've been wasting my time?"

"I'm not saying that."

"Well I'm hearing it. Gemme a Southern Comfort, double, on the rocks."

She handed me a twenty spot, with a flash of her eyes that obviated argument.

"It's up to you," I said, taking the note.

"No kidding," she replied, lighting a cigarette. "And, yeah, I'm smoking another, and I may's well snort Charlie and stick a spike in me, as if anyone gives a shit."

She continued in this vein while I waited to be served.

"And don't start thinkin' derogatory shit about me, 'cause I can read your mind, Billy, remember?"

The landlord glanced over my shoulder as he took the money.

"And it's not much of a read, as it goes," continued Joo-Lee. "Sort of like the funny pages, with silly people."

She stubbed out a half-smoked cigarette and scrabbled in the pack for another.

I pushed her drink across the table and she bent forwards and sipped from the surface while her hands busied themselves with cigarette and lighter. She flipped the fag lipwards and lit.

"That's good," she said, exhaling smoke.

She leaned forward, clenched the rim of the glass in her teeth, threw back her head and tossed off the liquor at one gulp.

"Nice trick," I said. "But don't you worry about the glass breaking?"

"It's only when you worry that it does. Get me another, will ya?"

The landlord put down his tabloid with an air of resentment.

"Same again, is it?" he asked.

"And another bitter."

"And another bitter," he repeated, turning to the task.

Joo-Lee joined me, looking along the rows of bottles at the back of the bar.

"I'd like to have a shot out of every one of them," she said.

"But have you the optic nerve to do it?"

The landlord pumped beer, the action seeming to sap his strength.

"That might be a bit expensive," he said.

"It's just money," replied Joo-Lee, handing him a fresh twenty.

"You wouldn't have anything smaller," he asked, glancing in my direction.

I began to feel in my pocket for change, but Joo-Lee pressed her hand on the front of my trousers.

"No, Billy, I insist," she said, smiling at the landlord and allowing him to pluck the note from her fingers. He held it up to the light, examining it scrupulously for several seconds, during which Joo-Lee gulped down her drink.

"Looks like I need a re-fill," she said, giggling. "You better take for another."

He had his back to us by now, fingers in the till. He stiffened, grabbed a glass, threw in ice, and sloshed in the spirit. Without a word, he placed the drink and the change on the bar, and resumed his newspaper.

"There are spirits all around us," giggled Joo-Lee, as we returned to our table.

"But you prefer them in a glass."

"Yeah, Bob Hope, 'The Cat and the Canary', good line, bad movie."

This reminded me of the old 'Carry On' film that was on TV the last time Jayne had come to see me.

"You know what's funny? The guy who owns the Hope is called Bob! Have you been in there lately?"

I pretended I hadn't heard her, swilling my beer.

We were the only customers. I could hear the pages turn as the landlord read his Sun. He glanced up through his eyebrows from time to time to monitor us, and I began to feel as though he wanted me to meet his eye. I kept mine down.

Joo-Lee was starting to talk louder, clowning a little with her glass, but Sun-man kept his weather eye on me. If there was going to be any bad pub behaviour, he obviously had me marked out as the one to blame.

The clincher was Joo-Lee noticing a smouldering dog-end in her ashtray, and trying to dive-bomb it with ice cubes.

The newspaper having been carefully folded and placed on the counter, I observed landlord's approach out of the corner of my eye. He walked as if weary from a long hike, stopping at our table and looking at us from behind large folded arms.

"Howdy!" said Joo-Lee.

He reached down and pulled the drink from her fingers.

"Out," he said.

I made to finish the rest of my beer, but he gripped my arm with hard fingers.

"I said out."

"Look, she didn't mean…"

He twisted my arm sharply behind my back, cutting me short.

"C'mon Billy, there's no use," said Joo-Lee, grabbing her cigarettes.

As she walked out, he frog marched me behind her, pushing me out onto the icy pavement.

"You want to keep control of that tart," he said, turning back into his establishment.

I watched him stroll over to our table. He picked up Joo-Lee's glass, sniffed the rim, and went round behind the bar. I felt a knot of resentment tightening in my stomach, unaware that Joo-Lee had started walking. Indignation rose in my guts, until I suddenly found I was hammering on the window with my fists. Landlord turned and started to run towards me. I could see his mouth opening and closing, but whatever he was shouting was suddenly obliterated by an explosive crack, as the glass gave way and shattered into thousands of flying fragments.

Joo-Lee stopped walking, and for a moment nobody moved.

"Little bastard," murmured the landlord.

I felt a warm trickle at my wrist, watched blood soak into my sleeve for a few seconds, and started to run.

Joo-Lee was beside me, grabbing at my jacket.

"Where're we goin'?" she kept shouting.

I was aware of the revving of a motor, squeal of rubber as a car scuddered into sudden motion. I knew it was him without looking back. So did Joo-Lee.

"Christ, Billy, he'll run us down, crazy motherfucker!"

She stopped and turned, smack in the middle of Rotherhithe Street, making mad gestures in the air with her fingers spread wide in front of her. Headlights shot her into silhouette, a gesticulating harpy.

The door of The Hope swung open and Declan came careering across the street, slopping pint of lager in one hand, grabbing Joo-Lee with the other.

"We need more like you," he yelled, dragging her backwards into the doorway.

The vehicle flashed past, brakes already screaming as the driver prepared to turn, and Declan seemed only then to spot me.

"Get in here very fucking rapidly," he shouted.

I did.

While Declan got busy bolting the door, Joo-Lee made a beeline for the optics.

Jayne came slowly from behind the bar, chalk pale.

"I'm dropping blood on the carpet," I said.

"Jesus, Billy, have you no consideration?"

She laughed slightly, pulling out a hanky.

"Come here, let's take a look."

She mopped at my wrist, and suddenly put her arms around me, holding tight.

"It doesn't look too bad," she whispered.

"Very touching sight," said Declan, "but what do we propose to do about the total psycho outside?"

We all stood listening for the sound of his vehicle.

"D'you think that door will hold out?" asked Joo-Lee, carrying over a tray of shots.

"You don't think he'll drive into it do you?" said Jayne.

"Just ice cubes in an ashtray," sighed Joo-Lee, as if about to read us one of her poems.

"I think," said Declan, chasing his drinks, "that we're dealing with one careless owner who's lost any respect he may have once had for his vehicle."

There was a rush of revving, tyres burning.

"I'm for calling the rozzers," said Jayne.

"Jesus!" said Declan, "you just sounded exactly like my mother."

We heard a muffled acceleration followed by silence.

"He's after getting an axe or something," hissed Jayne.

"Thanks for that," remarked Declan, refilling his pint glass.

"I'm gonna huff, and I'm gonna puff," growled Joo-Lee.

"That's exactly what *I'm* gonna do," said Declan, licking the edge of a Rizla.

"I don't suppose anyone has a plaster or something?" I asked.

"You'll have to have a tetanus," said Jayne, fiddling with my sleeve.

"What happened, anyway, Billy?" asked Declan.

"A difference of opinion."

"An asshole of a patron," said Joo-Lee.

"Some asshole."

"Maybe he's armed," remarked Jayne.

"Yeah, he'll be back with a fucking sawn-off, I don't think," said Declan with a snigger. "Mind you…"

He went to the window and peered through a gap in the boards, almost immediately ducking away.

"Keep down!"

After a few minutes, during which we all found ourselves crouching in ridiculous attitudes behind a table, eyes on the door, there came a rattling at the latch.

"Does Bob keep a baseball bat or anything?" whispered Declan.

"He's got a baseball cap," said Jayne.

"That's a comfort," said Declan.

Footsteps sounded outside the window, followed by a fist pounding on the door. Nobody moved.

The banging suddenly ceased, and after a short silence, somebody slowly lifted the letterbox.

"It's too early for a lock-in, so does somebody want to let me in on the joke?"

"Fucking Max!" said Declan.

He cautiously let him in, before re-bolting the door.

"Very cloak and dagger," said Max. "I take it you lot are somehow involved in what's happened out there."

We all stared at him.

"Oh, come on, don't play the innocent! Someone ploughs a Rover into the side of Lavender dock, and you know nothing about it?"

Declan was the first out, pupils dilated, with Joo-Lee a close second. Jayne hung back with Max and me.

"Is anyone actually working in here today?" asked Max.

"Serve yourself," said Jayne.

She took hold of my arm, guiding me to a corner.

"Where've you been? You never come in any more. Too good for us now are you, with your job and everything? I heard you got married. Is that her?"

"I haven't been anywhere, I'm not too good for anyone, I haven't got everything, I didn't, and that isn't."

She laughed, but looked sad.

"What am I gonna do, Billy? I don't know if I want to marry Declan. 'For better or worse.' I keep thinking there might be too much of the worse."

"He's alright."

"Yeah, he's a really nice guy, and all. A bit weird, but basically sound."

"I think he just saved my life."

"And hers."

"Joo-Lee."

"Yeah, Joo-Lee. She seems nice too."

"She is. A bit wired, but basically..."

The door swung open.

"There's nobody in the vehicle," reported Declan.

"But there's some blood on the dash!" added Joo-Lee.

"The car's totalled," Declan informed us with a grin.

"He must have been ok to walk away," said Jayne.

"I don't care if he is or isn't," said Joo-Lee, sitting next to Max and putting her arm around him.

"I've obviously missed something," he observed.

"Nothing much," said Declan, helping himself to whisky. "Just some hare-brained hot-wheels trying to spread this girlie over the tarmac."

"I coulda stopped him," said Joo-Lee, eyes gleaming.

"I think a speeding Rover 2000 might just have had the edge."

"Telekinetic energy," said Joo-Lee. "My power to force him off the road."

"Listen to *Carrie!*" said Max, but he squeezed her arm and smiled.

"It's what's in me," said Joo-Lee, staring into her drink.

"I'm going back to see if there's anything in the car worth nicking," said Declan. "Anyone care to join me?"

"I think I may have to relinquish my tenancy," sighed Max. "This area is going *so* downhill."

"Totally," nodded Joo-Lee.

"You'd come with me, wouldn't you sweetie?"

"Sure Maxy."

Jayne came away from the window, through which she had been half anxiously watching Declan.

"He's only after trying to open the boot! He can be such an idiot."

"He's pretty resourceful," I said. "Fixed my electricity."

"He has his uses. What I was saying earlier, Billy, what would you do?"

"I don't think I could marry Declan. I mean, I respect him…"

"Come on, can't you be serious with me?"

I didn't answer.

"Can you?"

"Yes!" came a shout from the street. "Merciful mother of God, there's almost a full case of whisky."

Adults Afloat

Astonishing news came on a postcard from Ted the bass player.

'I got us a gig. Probably no money, but we're supporting Billy Bragg. It's a miner's benefit at the Merlin's Cave. Give us a call.'

I was late for work, so I wouldn't get a chance to call Ted till lunchtime, or maybe in a tea break.

"What's a gig?" asked Brian, as we wheeled a patient called Mrs Moody to theatre.

"Don't you know?" laughed Austin.

"Why does it take three of us to assist this patient?"

Austin sloped off.

"It's a sort of concert," said Mrs Moody.

The Merlin's Cave turned out to more of a basement club.

"There's nothing magic about this dump," moaned Mary. "We're bound to mess it up, we don't know the songs."

"That's the spirit," said Steve.

"It'll be sound," said Ted.

I was still assembling my kit. Somehow it never looked quite right. Most of the cymbals were cracked, and the snare skin looked like the surface of the moon.

We were allowed a perfunctory sound check, before the sound system began pumping some ribcage rattling dub.

I went to the bar and a woman with a daisy drawn on her forehead served me a pint.

"When you're ready, flower," said a man standing next to me.

He was older than most of the crowd, and very skinny. Bony wrists jutted from the sleeves of his too-small jacket as he snapped open his storm-proof and lit up. His hair was 'Tru-Gelled' into a sleek quiff, long narrow sideburns accentuating the hollowness of his cheeks.

Catching my eye, he moved close, face level with mine, thumbs stuck into the pockets of his small black waistcoat. He exhaled from the corner of his mouth, and extended an arm, fingers slightly shaking.

On the fastener of his bootlace tie were a dancing couple in chrome. They came to life, bobbing on his adam's apple as he addressed me.

"Bluddy Rich!" he announced.

"Is it?"

"Is *I*, son. B. Rich, in person. Star of stage and, well, stage."

It rang a bell, but not a loud one.

"Yeah," he continued, "I was nearly famous. Used to M.C. 'The compere incomparable' they called me."

He dropped his cigarette, and, as he stooped to retrieve it, a lock of hair almost blue with grease flopped over his eyes.

"Oh yeah, I did a lot of them punk gigs, the early stuff. That's how I started, got a bit elephant's one night and did a stage raid. Introduced a lot of acts. I started throwing in a bit of improvised stuff."

He extended his arms, fingers outstretched, and exaggerated his East End accent.

"A man of extremes, a man for all reasons, whatever the means, no matter what season, let's here the next turn commit musical treason."

He laughed, setting off a volley of hacking coughs, which he soothed with a deep suck from his can of Special Brew, emptying it to the last and crumpling the aluminium between determined fingers.

"Smoke?" he said, holding out a pack of Marlboro.

I passed.

"Good boy. I can't quit. Chain fashion."

He inhaled deeply.

"You see this?"

He pushed hair back from his forehead to reveal a thin white scar running from hairline to eyebrow.

"That's where I was bottled, could of lost an eye, son. I usually went down well though."

With a long index finger, stained brown with nicotine, he pointed at the stage.

"I could get up and give you some build-up."

He did, and nobody threw any bottles. Nobody seemed to notice him, actually, and the 'Adults' went on to a similar reaction.

"I wonder why we fucking bother," said Mary as we packed up.

"Billy, who was that bloke you were talking to who got on stage?" asked Steve.

I told them about Bluddy.

"I saw him on 'The Tube' once," said Ted.

"I don't think I want to do this anymore," mumbled Mary.

"He was never on telly," said Steve. "You're thinking of John Cooper Clarke."

"Don't be a prat, he's totally different. He's from Salford."

"I can't see any point in it," concluded Mary.

Work at the hospital had settled into a comfortably predictable routine. Austin was easy to work with, as long as the T.A. wasn't mentioned, and he had an entertaining store of unlikely stories.

It was the day he brought in his set of erotic photographs that I realised just how delusional a man he was.

Brian had been goading him about the matter for weeks, little reminders, casual references to Pirelli calendars and 'Page Three', until, one snowbound afternoon, Austin cracked.

"Fuck this, man!" he shouted. "You don't deserve to see my work."

"Steady," countered Brian. "Don't chuck a mickey!"

"Don't tell me what to chuck. You wouldn't know talent if it came up and bit you."

The sky had been dark and still all day, and suddenly the white flakes descended, cascading past the window and gathering on the sill.

"Hark at David Bailey," said Brian.

"You know nothing. You wait, you'll see on Monday," answered Austin.

We did.

Brian was making instant coffee when Austin sauntered in late. He flopped a set of prints on the Formica tabletop, and strolled outside for a cigarette.

Brian glanced at me.

"After you, boss," I said.

He flipped through the pictures, his smile gradually subsiding, and shook his head slightly as he handed them over.

Although poorly focussed, they were obviously photographs of the pages of magazines. In some, the edge of the page was in shot, and on one I could just make out the staples on the crease.

"Christ," said Brian.

He lit a cigarette, in spite of the no smoking policy.

"Kid should get out more."

We glanced out to see if Austin was watching us, but he had already gone off to the wards.

"Never seen him get down to it so quickly," remarked Brian, putting the photographs back in their sleeve.

The stairwell was choked with the exhaled breath of furtive smokers.

I found Austin there, sharing a step and a fag with an old man in a tartan dressing gown who I thought looked vaguely familiar, but I couldn't think why. He was just reaching the concluding verse of a warbling rendition of 'Donald, where's your trousers?'

"You're my pal," I heard him tell Austin, before shuffling off.

"You've a friend there," I remarked.

"He's a loony toon, loves everyone and hates 'em too. Where're my photos?"

"Brian still has them."

"I'm getting tired of him, takes the piss too much. He used to be all right, for a batty. What do you think?"

"He's a pretty good bloke."

"No, man. The pictures."

"Oh, yeah. Professional job, I'd say."

"Try telling that to Brian."

"I will."

"Right. I'm off to get my pictures."

He stepped on the dog end of his cigarette, grinding ash into the concrete step.

The boy of spex

"I've been wearing glasses for as long as I can remember," said Declan. "Longer, in fact, 'cause I had 'em as a baby. Used to throw them out of my pram, so my parents tell me. Even they can't remember when I first had a pair. It wouldn't surprise me if I was born with them on, pink National Health frames, formed in the womb."

"That I think your parents *would* remember. Your mother at any rate," remarked Jayne.

"True. Anyway, these days I heard they can do scans, so you can see the baby before it's out."

"Useful," I said. "You'd know in advance if your child was going to come out wearing glasses."

"Four eyes is fore warned," added Jayne.

"They could probably perform some sort of surgery," said Declan. "A speccyotomy."

Max was fiddling with a Star Wars game that Bob had recently installed.

"Your drivel is putting me off my stroke," he complained, stabbing furiously at several plastic buttons, his face bluish from the glare of the screen.

"It's you that's putting *us* off with that crappy fucking machine," countered Declan. "There should be bar billiards and dominoes only."

"Oh drag yourself into the twentieth century," said Max, smacking the side of the machine as his time ran out.

He came over to the bar and bought us drinks.

"I shouldn't be buying for you," he said, raising his glass to me. "Not now you're working. What about you, Declan, any prospect of a bit of the old gainful?"

"Nah, I'm the unemployable man. There are barge poles being specially made for employers not to touch me with."

"You could get a job making them."

"Ah, but if I was working, the demand for the poles would cease, and I'd be made redundant."

I nodded.

"Exactly. It wouldn't make sense for the manufacturers to employ the very man whose unemployed status ensures the continued sale of the poles."

"I don't believe this," said Jayne, slapping a tea towel on the bar.

"I hope they're using wood from sustainable forests," said Max.

"I really don't," said Jayne.

A loose end to a lost afternoon.

Oh, Joe

The hospital job's trial period passed and I was a porter proper, attending to patients under the supervision of Brian.

As well as Austin, I worked with a woman called Brenda, who consistently started her shifts by reiterating how much she hated the job, and Iain, nicknamed Inane, who wore bottle-thick glasses that made his eyes look tiny.

"The frames have to be specially made, on account of the weight of the lenses," he told me.

Austin was the self appointed cock of the wards. He seemed to think his T.A. training qualified him for seniority over us. He also talked behind their back about anyone, especially those who didn't attend our regular Thursday evening sessions at the Prince of Wales.

"You're alright, Billy, a bit weird, but basically ok. I do *not* know what is going on with Inane, I mean the guy is so out there he's gonna have a hard time comin' back, you know what I mean? And Bender, Jesus, man, she's *married*, you know! I mean what can the husband be like, you know what I'm sayin'?"

Such comments were usually concluded with much laughter and finger popping.

"No-one comes up to your standards," commented Brian over his Fosters, one Wales night.

"Meaning?" asked Austin.

"Well, you know, we can't all be Rambo, Man Ray and hospital porter of the month, can we?"

"You're ridin' close to the wind, my friend."

"I didn't know you took an interest in poetry, Austin," said Bernard, polishing a glass and holding it up to the light.

"What makes you think I do?"

"Oh, it was just Brian's reference to Rimbaud."

"I'll tell you what," said Austin, "whatever you lot are on, I wouldn't mind having some of it."

"I find *'Le bateau ivre'* most striking," said Bernard.

"It's your round Billy," said Austin.

I often didn't see much of Max or Jim for weeks, and when Max was around he usually stayed in his room most of the time. Joo-Lee had also taken to staying out, sometimes for several days. She often returned with only vague recollections of where she had been.

"Oh, you know, Billy, just here and there, up and down."

I was sitting in the flat one afternoon wondering how long it was since I had spoken to anyone apart from at work, when Joe called by.

"Sorry to be out of touch so long," he said, offering a strip of gum. "I've been trying to sort out the Alison thing."

"It's Alison, now, is it?"

"Is with me."

"Things ok?"

"Yeah, pretty good. She's started going out with Emma. You know, really little girl, you talked to her at a party."

"Brave Emma."

"Tell me! Anyway, I'm well off the hook. Enough about that, I was wondering if Peter and me could drop by this evening?"

"Peter?"

He twisted some of his ear studs.

"Yeah, you know, we've been hanging out a bit. He's nice. Been a bit lonely."

"Ok, I'm not going anywhere."

"Good. We've had an idea for a sort of game."

"What sort of sort of game?"

"You'll see."

With that he was off.

I read the graffiti on the living room wall.
'Don't just sit there, go out and do life!'
It was there when we moved in.

When Joe returned, he had a carrier bag full of cans and bottles, and a rolled up wall atlas under his arm.
"No Peter?" I asked.
"He'll be along after work. He likes to get out of his suit," answered Joe, spreading out the map on the floor, and getting beers out of the bag.
"Tell me," I said, "does this game of yours' involve nudity in any way?"
He grinned, screwing round a silver stud in his cheek.
"Billy! What do you take me for?"
He took a wad of gum from his mouth and stuck down a stubborn corner of the map.
"I mean, apart from anything, can you imagine Peter stripping off?"
I tried not to.
"That's probably him now."
He went to the door, leaving me with the world at my feet.
"Hope you don't mind this imposition?" said Peter.
"Let's play," said Joe. "It's a drinking voyage thing. Every country we visit, we have the appropriate drink, and put one of these on to show we've been."
He waved a little packet of coloured stickers.
"Cheaper than Thompson's," I said.
"Only just," said Peter. "The price of some of these imported beers…"
"It's just a laugh," said Joe.
He unscrewed a bottle of Bells.
"May as well start in Scotland."
"I'm not sure how well I'll travel," I said. "I'm on an early tomorrow."
Max came in, dropping his suitcase.
"Madhouse, utter madhouse. Carries on like this and I'm resigning. Oh, Peter, lovely surprise! Jim's not here, but I'm meeting him later at some unsavoury club. Welcome to join us."
"Actually, I'm here with Joe."
"Oh, Joe."
Joe explained the game.
"Talk about cruising for a boozing," said Max.
He wagged a finger at me.
"Think of your career, Billy, don't let them take you further than Skeggie."
As it turned out, I spent most of my time in Scotland.
Joe and Peter covered some miles though.
"Joe, care to join me for a spot of ouzo?"
"We haven't got any ouzo."
"Bugger! Never mind, I'm sticking a spot on anyway. I've always fancied Lesbos."
"Come here and I'll give you a red stripe."
"Not sure I like the sound of that."
I started to nod, drowsy with the scotch, so I cried off.
Next morning my head was clanging.
"The Bells!" shouted Max, quasi-dancing around me as I tried to make coffee.
"I warned you, but you wouldn't listen. Silly Billy."

As he left, he started to sing.

"Heigh ho, heigh ho, it's off to work I go, with a bucket and spade and a hand grenade…"

I wished I had one.

Peter and Joe were asleep in the living room, the atlas, covered in stickers and stains, draped over them.

I quietly closed the door and had my coffee in the kitchen.

Still no sound from the living room when I left for work.

Approaching the tube station, I spotted Joo-Lee, whee, girl on a bicycle, zooming along short sockedly. She hurtled on, panting over the pedals, oblivious to my shout of recognition. I started to run, gaining ground as she slowed behind a bus, but she swerved out to pass it, leaving me gasping fumes.

As the bus pulled away, I caught sight of her again, halted by a busy roundabout. She was trying to edge forwards, but a driver had brought his van to a halt in front of her. He wound down his window for a better view.

"You stupid cow," he shouted. "I hope you have an accident."

"You *are* an accident, pecker brain."

Was she tired of life?

I caught up just as the van door swung open, and the driver jumped out. He fixed me with red-rimmed eyes.

"What are you lookin' at?" he asked.

Before I could answer, Joo-Lee bumped her bike up onto the pavement beside me.

"Hop on, Sundance!" she yelled, offering me her handlebars.

The odds were long, but somehow we pulled it off, leaving vanman shouting himself puce above a cacophony of horns.

"Fucking Yahoo!" shouted Joo-Lee, laughing, swerving.

"I'm due in at the hospital," I protested.

"Sorry, man, we don't stop at no hospital, no sir, we is express. Anyhow you don't look ill to me, baby."

"I work there, remember?"

She pedalled harder, shifting through the gears. She was a skilful cyclist, but I felt we were riding for a fall.

Work was looking faded.

She suddenly braked, precipitating me neatly onto the pavement in front of a telephone box.

"Call sick," she said. "We have some catching up to do."

So I was back home, another day's work undone.

We sat in the living room, and every time I went to say something Joo-Lee stopped me.

"It's ok, Billy," she said, pressing her temples with her fingertips. "I'm getting most of it anyway."

So much for catching up.

I started tidying up instead, binning bottles and cans, flotsam and jetsam from Joe and Peter's round the world booze.

Joo-Lee picked up the crumpled atlas.

"What's all this about?" She asked. "I can't connect with it."

"Oh, just a game."

"The games people play, eh Billy?"

She passed her hand across the land and the sea.

"Maybe that's exactly what the world is, after all. Just one big silly game."

The next morning Joo-Lee turned to me.

"Why do people's ears get bigger when they get old?" she asked, fiddling with her lobes.

"They don't. It's the head shrinking that gives that impression."

"Don't talk balls," intervened Max, coming from his room in shirt and socks. "If the cranium shrank, the face would fall off."

"Which it sorta does, I guess," replied Joo-Lee.

"Speak for yourself, girlfriend! How the hell are you?"

"I'm good. Hey, it's been far too long."

"Still is darling! Come on, give us a kiss, tell us what you've been up to."

They went to his room, and I listened to the murmur of conversation, punctuated by occasional hoots and squawks from Max.

I went for a quick lie down before work.

I got to the hospital late.

Brian frowned at me over his reading glasses.

"Austin covered your early," he said, resuming his perusal of the Express.

My rota had gone out the window. One bike-riding madwoman, like a spanner in the cog.

"He's waiting for you, mate."

Austin raised an eyebrow, and sent a bundle of laundry spinning across the corridor.

"You can take over for me, I'm going for a smoke."

I began to apologise.

"NO need, man, no need. We look after each other, you know what I mean? You might be able to help me out some day."

He levelled a fist at my chest, which I clumsily knocked with mine.

"Sweet," he said, chuckling.

I stooped to gather up the bedding

"First round on you tonight, Brenda!" said Brian.

It was coffee break.

"You know I'd love to come, Bri, but Colin hates me stopping out. He doesn't really approve of women in pubs."

"What's he like?" asked Austin. "You have to have barmaids don't you?"

"I think he means ladies not there in a professional capacity," suggested Iain.

"Come to think of it, there's hardly ever any women in the Prince, have you noticed that?" observed Austin.

"Can't say I have," said Brian.

"You coming tonight, Billy?" asked Austin.

Thursday again.

"I suppose so," I replied.

"Christ," said Brian, "don't let's all get too carried away! Iain, Brenda, you were due back ten minutes ago."

"I bloody hate this job," said Brenda.

Austin left early to go to a pool hall, and I was rushing around trying to finish his work, and catch up with mine, when I collided with a solidly built senior consultant.

He stooped to pick up some trays I had been carrying.

"No harm done," he said, handing them to me.

He adjusted some pens in his breast pocket, and, as he proceeded, lowered his left hand and lightly tickled my balls in passing.

Basket case Britain

I got home later than ever.

I was working over my time, but I wasn't getting paid any overtime.

"Your dinner's in the pub," yelled Joo-Lee.

I used to find her so cute when she was drunk.

I made something from spaghetti and tomato paste, which Joo-Lee said looked like entrails.

"What fate will they augur?" I murmured.

"I'll tell you one thing that's gonna happen," said Joo-Lee. "They're gonna close down Fleet Street and print all the papers on computers, and have colour pictures and shit. A lot of people aint gonna get no fish and chip supper tonight. The terrorism of technology."

She retrieved a cigarette from behind her left ear, fitting it between her lips and sucking smoke at the first flare of the lighter.

"So? Colour pictures are alright, aren't they?"

"That's so way off the point, baby. It's about jobs, sweetie, machines doin' people's work, all the presses falling silent."

"Where do you get all this from?"

"I know things, I told you before. It's gonna come down, just like I say. Hey, I went to the tattoo parlour, just like it said in that message I had the other night. You remember that don't you? Sure you do. Oh, man, I can't believe I didn't show you it yet!"

She pulled up the sleeve of her shirt, one of mine, and twisted her skinny arm to reveal an ink-etched trail, from underarm to wrist, reading,

'Everything is ultimately dissapointing.'

"Very nice," I said. "They've misspelled disappointing."

She stared at it.

"No shit? Well…see…that just totally endorses the philosophy!"

"No pictures?" I asked.

"You're such a baby, Billy. Wait till Max gets back, he'll understand."

She frowned, pouty.

"You're so mean all of a sudden, Billy-o."

She dragged a half empty bottle of wine from behind a cushion and splashed some into a pint glass already containing brandy.

The room smelled of stale smoke, ash, sweat, warm socks, cat piss, liquor.

"Cheers, Billy!" said Joo-Lee, smiling sideways.

I noticed there were fibres of tobacco floating on the surface of her drink.

Max shimmied in, his overcoat whirling around him like Bela Lugosi's cape.

"Hello, loves!" he trilled. "Uh-oh, I detect a nettled young man and a pickled female. Come on J, come to Uncle Max!"

She held out her arms like a toddler playing baby.

"My God, J, and other people's, what in *Hell?* You've been decorated! I didn't think you'd go straight out and do it! I mean…"

Without the slightest movement of her head, Joo-Lee raised her eyes until they were almost engulfed by their sockets, knitting her brows, dark and low.

"Hey, I'm not saying I don't like it, angel, its just a little bit of a surprise. Let's see."

"Cross her arm with silver first."

"Yes, well thank you, Billy. If you've nothing constructive to say you can get us all a drink. I've got some vodka in my briefcase, and there had better be some ice left."

"Yes Sir, ice detail, on the double."

"Just fix the fucking drinks, strange boy. Now, illuminated lady, give me your arm."

I went to the hall where Max always drops his case.

It lay, jaws ajar, just inside the front door. Ferreting out the Red Square, I noticed a cellophane packet containing several small pills, which I stole. There was also a small book among Max's files. *His* book. Slipping this into my back pocket, I went and mixed Max a huge one, leaving him toying with Joo-Lee's arm, herself screeching with alternate laughter and pain as he pawed and recited.

Installed in my room, I once more separated the pages of Dr Max's Nutcasebook. On several pages the text had been scored through as if in regret. I flicked through nervously, looking for Rothman, and came upon a capital J, with a squiggly biro flourish beneath.

'She's actually sort of horny, when she's not totally out there. Can't tell if she's straight. Goes out with Billy, but I'm not sure that counts. She's still unwell. Shrink thinks otherwise, mentioning attention-seeking, usual guff. I should have their salary! She is…"

I turned the page.

No more on Joo-Lee.

I slipped the book back in the briefcase, but absconded with the drugs, the sound of Max and J giggling in my ears.

Outside it was chucking it down and they were chucking them out.

I sidled past the Hope, lights visible through the chinks in the boards, and went to the Ship and Whale, a gay bar that had a late licence.

I had enough money for a pint o' piss.

After a couple of sips, I went for leak, and as I zipped up, I heard the package of pills spill.

A few rattled urinalwards.

I scooped up the rest and popped them, a bitter taste frothing on my tongue, which I washed down at the bar with a gulp of Castlemaine. Behind the bar, a couple of young men started parading around wearing nothing but their underpants.

This was unusual, even for the S & W.

"It's 'Mr Capital Gay'," explained the barman, tossing over a thin tabloid.

The give-away fagrag was running pub heats to find the tastiest fellow in pants.

"I can't seem to whip up much enthusiasm," he complained. "Surely it's worth a try? Winner gets fifty quid."

Maybe this was why my Mum used to go on about wearing clean underpants.

I stumbled into the ring, self consciously flexing my arms where there ought to be muscles, raised an amused cheer, and came second.

I won an alarm clock.

"Time, gentlemen, please."

I couldn't stop laughing.

Someone bought me a pint, and I tried to pull my trousers up with one hand while holding the drink in the other. It didn't occur to me to put it down.

The barman was whispering something. To me. Something he repeated like a hissing mantra. It got louder.

"Part your tweeds, part your tweeds!"

It was like Chinese whispers.

"Parts of weeds," I said, leaning on a small man with a walrus moustache. He moved away.

Someone tried to tie my laces for me. His lips moved but he made no sense.

Too much echo.

Oscillating coloured lights…

I'm in Rotherhithe Street, and there's Sir Marc Brunel, dancing around a stovepipe hat.

"Jimmy Savile for Queen!" he calls out.

Clive James punches him, before commencing an elaborate ballet manoeuvre with an Algerian girl wearing only a baby-doll nightie. The girl is wearing even less.

They are applauded by Leonard Cohen, who growls, "the future is a dirty old man, jacking off inside his raincoat, 'mid the stink of nicotine and come."

He takes a cloak from the shoulders of a zombie Janis Joplin and throws it over my head, but I still hear her hysterical laughter.

"Max, over here," comes Joo-Lee's shimmering voice.

Her head blends with Max's.

"You silly, silly arse."

Max was leaning over me, hands on hips, slowly shaking his head.

My tongue felt like a loofah.

"If you *want* something, you should talk to me. I thought I was going to have to call an ambulance. That would not be good, Billy. Lots of questions. Not something I need, all right? Here, drink some."

He handed me a cup of tea.

"Thanks, but I better go and call work."

"It's ok Billy, you're sick today. I called for you. It's half past three in the afternoon."

"Not again. Is Joo-Lee here?"

"She got a bit freaked out. She's uncomfortable around people when they're…not themselves."

"As if *she* never is."

"She feels threatened. I've worked with her, remember?"

I nodded.

"That's it, sport, don't talk too much. Have your tea, have a biccy. I have to go tend to the headsick, but J should be back soon. She went out on her bike, clear her head. See you later."

I lay staring at the ceiling, seeing animal shapes in the cracks and damp patches, and was just starting to doze when a sharp repetitive noise snatched me back. It was coming from the pile of my clothes at the side of the bed.

From the inside pocket of my jacket, I pulled the cheap alarm clock, and depressed the button.

I went into the living room, where large cat was asleep, spread on the mattress like peanut butter. The smell of spray sent me out onto the balcony, and it was from there I noticed the ambulance. They carried Vic out on a stretcher, a sort of bag covering his body.

The cat sauntered up behind me, stretching.

"Looks like you're here to stay," I remarked.

He put his head out, sniffed the rain, and hurried back inside.

I went to the Hope, where Declan was declaiming.

"A jackboot stamping on the collective head of humanity. Mr Potato-head, mashed. All those chips off the old bloke! I'm drunk, by the way."

Jayne pulled me a pint.

"Don't encourage him," she implored. "He's been waffling on about potatoes for the past hour."

"I wouldn't think of it."

He waved.

"You two are talking about me in a conspiratorial fashion. Hey! Maybe I'm not as thought as I drunk I was."

"Ignore him," said Jayne. "D'you fancy coming with me to the Bell after I finish?"

"The Bell?"

"It's a club in Kings Cross."

Declan scoffed.

"It's one of them places where they ask if you're gay before they let you in. What am I gonna say, 'no, boss, I'm a queer basher?'"

"You probably would," said Jayne. "They're just trying to catch out the pretty police."

Declan slapped a palm to his forehead.

"Now who's talking shite? When did you ever see a pretty peeler? Fascists to a man. For mash get smashed!"

"For God's sake," murmured Jayne. "Please let it be last orders."

"Do you ever hear anything from Liz?" shouted Jayne above the Bronski Beat in the Bell.

"No. She's gone I suppose."

"Do you miss her?"

"I do sometimes. She burns her bridges."

"And you don't?"

"You never know when you might need 'em."

"Do you want to dance?"

"Not much."

"What do you want to do?"

"Sit with you and answer your questions."

"Why don't you ask me something?"

"Like what?"

"There, you did it."

She was right, though, I wasn't good at asking.

She suddenly got up and hit the dance floor with some wild flailing of arms. A woman with pockmarked cheeks, wearing a cap with a chain on it moved in close. She was beautiful in a sinewy, Donald Duck kind of way, circling, and aping Jayne's moves. She said something very close to Jayne's ear, and was given the requested light for her King-Size. Jayne glanced at me, and danced on.

I realised I had never seen her dance. I hadn't seen her do much, apart from keeping the Hope, and Declan, together.

The music started shifting into another tune, and Cap-girl was talking close again. Jayne smiled, shaking her head, at which the woman kissed her own forefinger, pressed it to Jayne's lips, and shimmied away.

Jayne waved, beckoning me to join her, so I went over and we threw a few shapes. She laughed, shouting in my ear.

"You dance in such a weird way!"

"It's taken me years of practice."

"Unnatural practice."

"In some countries it's considered beautiful."

"On some planets, more like."

She took me home to her cold flat, and we got under her threadbare blankets. She went spark out, but I felt restless. There was something bothering me, a nothing that grew in the night, like a slowly inflated balloon.

"Jayne," I said.

She turned, sleepy.

"Mmm?"

"What did that woman want?"

She half-opened her eyes.

"Woman, what woman?"

"She was dancing with you."

"Oh, she needed a light."

"No, later. She asked you something."

"Did she?"

"I saw you shake your head. What did she want?"

"I don't know. Try to sleep."

"She asked you to go with her, didn't she?"

"Billy, don't do this, will you?"

"Is that what *she* wanted? To do it?"

"Now you're being absurd."

"Am I? She did, didn't she? Ask you to go with her?"

She sat up.

"Yes, yes, she asked me to go home with her! And I said no. Satisfied?"

"Did you want to?"

"For God's sake, Billy, please! I don't want to remember us like this. Why would I go off with some woman all of a sudden when it's just a few weeks to my wedding?"

"Last fling?"

"Billy, you're my last fling, can't you see that?"

She lay back, staring at the moonlight on the ceiling.

"I'm sorry," I said. "I just feel so ridiculously tired. I don't think having a job really suits me."

"Maybe you just haven't found the right one?"

"Maybe."

"Are you ok?"

"I think so."

"I think so too."

I only just made my shift on time next morning, unshaven and crumpled.

"Look what the cat dragged in!" said Brian, cheery. "Feeling better, mate?"

"Just sort of flu or something. I got a certificate, but I forgot it."

"No worries. You sure you're right over it? You don't look so hot."

"I think so. There's a few things at home I'm sort of trying to sort out."

"Any time you want a chin wag, you don't have to wait for supervision."

"Thanks…"

"Open door policy."

Brenda came in.

"See what I mean?"

"Weekends," she complained. "Why did God have to make Saturdays and Sundays shorter than the other days? I don't know what I'm doing here."

"I'll tell you," said Brian. "You're going out on a biscuit run. Lemon puffs. Billy, you can help me with Mr Groody."

We took a wheelchair to the patient's bed. He was a tall man, wearing flannelette pyjamas, propped up against a lot of pillows. He had his arms folded, and refused to look at us.

"Come on, mate," said Brian. "Your chair awaits."

"I aint your mate, and it aint right you moving me about like this. I'm supposed to be recovering."

Brian's eye flickered at me.

"Never mind, we don't make the rules…"

"Yes, I know, just following instructions. There was a lot of men lost in the War for that, I can tell you. You're not from round here are you?"

Brian smiled.

"No, I'm an aboriginal homosexual. Now, shall we get you up and into the wheel chair?"

"I can do that much myself. It was my ears what they done, not my legs."

"Perhaps you'd prefer to walk?" I suggested.

"Don't be a fool, I've got bad feet."

He grumbled all the way.

"Mind that DOOR! Watch out you fool! Don't they give you no TRAINING?"

Brian kept nudging me, red faced with barely suppressed mirth, but as we were going down in the lift he fell silent, supporting himself by the handle of the chair. He keeled sideways to the floor. At the bottom, I dragged him out and sat him against the wall. He was pale, shivering and yawning.

I called out for help, and a junior doctor hurried over. I watched him loosen Brian's tie and collar, and heard, too late, muffled cries of indignation as the lift doors closed on Mr Groody and he was borne up to another part of the building.

There she goes again

"What now my love?" sang Jim to Max.

"Have you finished chopping the tomatoes and peppers?"

"Mais oui."

"Well grate some cheese or something."

"There is no greater love!"

"God you're irritating sometimes! Can't you improvise?"

"Not really, I'm just a singer, standard lyrics, not an interpreter."

"Well just *cut* the fucking fromage, use a knife, slice it, dice it, whatever!"

Without comment, Jim scraped the finely chopped ingredients on to the pizza base, laid down the knife beside the board, wiped his hands on a tea towel, removed and hung up his apron, and walked quietly out of the kitchen.

Left looking at the half prepared meal, Max's face evinced a little twang of remorse. It didn't resonate, however, perhaps curtailed by the busy entrance of Joo-Lee, skeetering around on her flip-flops and slopping wine from a big teacup.

"You got any cigarettes?" she asked, close to Max's ear.

"I want some," he replied. "I think we should brave the cold and find some dark corner of a pub where we can sit and drink and smoke ourselves stupid."

Joo-Lee licked Max's earlobe.

"Sometimes I love you, baby, you make my heart leap."

"Well, boom-bang-a-bang, let's go," he answered.

I remained where I had been for the past two hours, crouched on the mattress in the living room watching Joo-Lee irritating the cat, and, through the serving hatch, Max and Jim making a meal of it in the kitchen.

Now they were all out of sight.

I had a go at tidying, and found some of Joo-Lee's wine supply wrapped in various garments in the airing cupboard.

She had started to secrete the sup.

I took a tepid gulp, flushing away the aftertaste of bad coffee and dry roasted peanuts, the best I could get when I went up to see Brian at Guys hospital.

He was recovering from a heart attack, a little sleepy and pale, but still kidding.

"What, no flowers?"

"I didn't think."

"I'm hurt. A few pansies would have been nice. How's things?"

I told him Austin had been temporarily put in charge, and he nearly choked on his water.

"Are you trying to give me a heart attack?"

There was a needle taped to his hand, a plastic tube leading up to a bottle.

"Don't worry, Billy mate. I'll soon be back to knock things into shape."

By the time Max and Joo-Lee returned, giggling, Jim had shared the pizza with me and gone to bed.

Max picked at a bit of crust.

"Nice of you to save me some," he said.

"We just saw some new folks moving in next door," remarked Joo-Lee.

"I'm not sure they're right for the area," said Max.

Joo-Lee laughed.

"What, not the right kind of squatter?"

Max handed her a quarter bottle of vodka.

"I'm just joking, dear."

She took a slug and sat on the floor to roll a joint.

Max took back the bottle.

"Mind you, they're all females, and they do look a bit Greenham Common if you ask me."

Joo-Lee scowled at him.

"Max, what the fuck?"

"Well, all those cropped heads and bovver boots."

"Don't wind us up," I said.

"It speaks!" remarked Max, laughing. "Anyway I couldn't care less, but they look like a gaggle of dykes to me."

"A gaggle?" repeated Joo-Lee."

"What *would* be the collective term for a group of lesbians A well, perhaps? A butch?"

He sat down next to me, offering the vodka.

"A rubyfruit, snatch, clam, a dildo?"

Joo-Lee suddenly threw the makings of her spliff at him.

"What the fuck does anyone care?" she yelled. "What the fucking shit does it matter who's coming to dinner?"

She stomped upstairs.

"Well, who twanged her clapper?" shrugged Max.

I went up after her.

She was rummaging under the bed on all fours, half undressed.

"Or half-dressed," she mumbled.

I couldn't think of a reply.

"Did you drink my wine?" she asked, her voice growing louder, higher. "I had some fucking hooch under here, *and* some God-damned grade-A, head-smackin', brain whackin' here comes Charley girl! Now all I see is dust and fluff. Well? Speak, fucker!"

"Ok, I drank some of your wine, but it wasn't under the bed, and I have no idea about the other crap you're talking about."

She surfaced, dusty.

"Yeah, sure. Sorry. Not too cool, y'all."

She sat up on the bed, small breasts pale and goose bumped, shaking her head around, shivering.

"Why don't you fuck me, Billy?" she murmured, raising herself to a kneeling stance and holding out her scrawny arms, long fingers, layers of translucent nail polish eroded to the quick.

I caught her tight and we fell clumsily across the bed.

She quickly went to sleep.

"Everything and everyone is grey at dawn," came a voice through my dreams.

"Morning, Joo-Lee."

Her warm smoker's mouth touched my ear.

"Good morning," she whispered.

"I'm not awake."

"Oh, sure, no one's a-fuckin' wake! We're all the living dead, man, crawling over the earth in search of a warm grave."

"Can this wait? I have to get up for work soon."

"Sure. You have to climb out of your tomb and go creepin', scratchin' for pennies, pickin' coins off of dead people's eyes! Yeah, you do it Billy, you just go and do what ever you feel compelled to do, go fuck corpses."

"Maybe later, eh?"

"Huh! Sure. When there's no room in hell, we walk the earth. Limbo land, baby, you know it. Purge-a-Tory. A little dead time story…tuck you in and suck you in…"

And then someone calling,

"Billy, Billy, wakey-wakey time, come on old sport, let's be having you!"

It was Max, gripping my shoulders.

"Come on, Billy!"

My head ached and the room felt cold.

"Billy," persisted Max, "you've missed work. I 'phoned in for you, favour returned once more."

"WHAT?"

"I thought you'd gone, then I heard snoring, looked in, there you are! Didn't have the heart to wake you, so I thought I'd nip out and make your excuses. Came back to check on you and saw that."

"What?"

"The window, chummy."

I peered over to where he was pointing. The pane was smashed.

"There's a spot of blood," said Max.

"On the window?"

"Well it's not on my hand, I'm hardly lady Macbeth. Yes, the window. Buck up Banquo, something's happened to Joo-Lee!"

I got dressed and we stood by the broken window.

"Aren't you being a bit of a drama queen?" I said. "It's just a window."

"Don't forget the blood. With Joo-Lee, nothing would surprise me. We'd better make an examination of the area below."

"Ok Sherlock."

"How can you be so flippant?"

I looked out.

"At least there doesn't seem to be anything down there."

"By 'anything' you mean Joo-Lee, I suppose?"

"Amazing deduction!"

"You know my methods. You don't actually think she jumped, do you?"

"What, and limped off somewhere, with a broken ankle or something?"

"I reckon she climbed down the gutter pipe, silly mare. We'll probably find her in the Hope."

But we didn't.

"Come on, Max," said Declan. "You must know how her mind works."

"Excuse me, but I'm not a shrink. Drink up, Billy, we'd better try her other haunts."

He took me to the Silverton Arms.

"I didn't know she went in here," I said.

"I've had the odd one with her. We have to be thorough, no stone unturned."

The pub was empty.

"Vodka and tonic and a pint of bitter," ordered Max.

"Er, why are you buying drinks?"

"Eh? Oh, she might be in the ladies."

"We could just have looked."

"Oh, no, Billy, one never looks in the ladies."

We sat near the toilets beneath a notice that read,

'Lord Silverton was temporarily deranged by the vast wealth he inherited.'

"I should go mad so," I murmured.

"Pardon, Billy?"

"Nothing. Look, Max, she's either not in there or she's having an almighty long…"

"Yes, thank you, Billy, point taken. I suggest we proceed to the Mayflower."

She wasn't there either, but he still got a round in.

"I can't believe this," I said. "It's turning into an excuse for a piss up."

"What's with the 'turning'? Anyway, we're in shock, we need something to calm our nerves."

We did the Ship next, and by the time we sat down in the Adam and Eve, any remaining sense of urgency had been thoroughly flushed away.

"Is there anything left to drink anywhere?" pleaded Max, as we stumbled back into the squat.

"You could try the airing cupboard."

He gave me his sympathy-for-the-imbecile look, so I went for him.

Any wine that remained was in Joo-Lee.

She was crammed in among the clothes, knees drawn up to her chin, the ripped sleeve of a shirt tied round her injured hand. She was awake but very drowsy. I tried to take her arm, but she shrugged me off.

"Who let you in here? My Daddy's gonna be awful mad."

Max was already on his way to the 'phone box.

In Here and Out There

A fly, big, dusty and dopey, was buzzing around the overheated Head Porter's office. Austin swiped at it with a rolled up newspaper, but his reactions weren't fast enough.

"Sooner or later I will get you," he asserted. "Now, Billy, as Brian is still not fit, it falls to me to give you supervision, right?"

"You tell me."

"Yeah, well, actually, this is sort of, like, the chance for you to tell me things."

"What things?"

He suddenly grabbed the paper truncheon and caught the insect a whack, sending it spiralling like a crippled spitfire. It lay still on the carpet.

"You know, about your work and that. I've noticed you've been a bit unreliable lately."

I would have preferred to discuss this with Brian.

"I've had a few worries."

"Well, let's talk."

"I'd like to make an appointment with the medical officer."

The fly started to move its legs.

"Oh, right, well, if that's what you want."

"Yes."

The fly was crawling now.

Austin scribbled in a folder.

"Alright, that's all. You going down the Prince on Thursday?"

"Not until Brian's back."

"Right."

As I left, I heard the buzzing start.

Joo-Lee was back on 'Red Team', Maudseley material once more.

She was refusing visitors, saying she knew no such persons, yet the first thing she did each morning was ask for Max. Naturally, he took pleasure in sharing this with me.

"We'll pull her through, love," he averred.

"I don't see how I come into it."

"Give it time. She needs a lot of T.L.C. I'll make sure she gets it."

"Has anyone contacted her parents?"

"That's what I wanted to ask you. She denies having a mother, but talks, a bit oddly, about her father. I wondered if you knew of any way we could contact him?"

"He sometimes sends money."

"Any note, a letter?"

"She never mentioned it."

"He must write something."

"I wouldn't know. Money comes, she spends it."

"Big help you are. Still, if you think of anything… I have to dash, Jim's got a gig. Ta-ra!"

I walked to Jayne's flat, but she wouldn't open the door. She said she had a bad case of flu.

As I wandered back, a tourist boat passed, tinny amplified voice of the guide carried on the breeze.

'…Mayflower's maiden voyage…historic pageant…reign of King Charles…'

A scrap of paper blew against my shoe, a young child's crayon drawing of a man, big scribbled eyes and stick fingers.

He fluttered from my hand, hit the water, and was borne briefly afloat before being sucked under.

Miles of Smiles

I was running, hip hop hopping along on a caffeine high, heading for karaoke night in a pub in Camberwell, where, on the mad-o-meter, the sing-along swung way into the red.

I built up a nice head of self-esteem, clattering down the escalator as a train sat waiting on the platform. As I neared, the doors closed, but the driver waved me over and let me ride up front. Hammering head-on into stations, passengers shuffling forward, I wondered if I was in the company of a suicidal lunatic. The way I was laughing, he probably did too.

At the Elephant and Castle, I caught a number twelve, and rode for free, evening sun on the top deck. Rippling, flitting light, a pall of smoke clinging to the ceiling like upside-down mist.

A voice in my head said 'a new sun is rising today!' Maybe it was someone on the bus. Or a headline.

Coffee-fuelled and careless, I blinked into the dark of the bar, where a middle-aged woman was half way through 'King of the Road', tinny microphone clutched tight.

I got a beer and found a seat next to a large black woman who was sucking her drink through a straw. She was up next and did a strident rendition of 'I will survive', mostly in tune, before returning to collapse laughing onto our bench of scarlet Dralon.

"That was good," I said.

"Thanks darlin', you want a drink?"

"Ok."

"In that case, mine's a Pernod and pineapple juice, with a straw."

She laughed as she shuffled a fiver from her purse, waving it towards me. She had long red nails, with tiny stick on jewels.

A man got up to perform 'Crying'. He held the mike in both hands, scraps of bandage wrapped around his fingers, word perfect with his back to the screen.

Jacky, my new friend, asked me to walk her home. She lived just off Coldharbour Lane in a flat that had motorcycle parts on sheets of newspaper in the hall.

We sat in her living room, and she made a big spliff, which I declined.

She smoked, growing garrulous.

"Shall I tell you how I met Barry? I'm walking home, right, and this massive truck pulls up and just literally brings the traffic to a halt, and there's this big bloke in the cab leaning out, and do you know what he asks me? He only asks where is Coldharbour Lane, right, and I say, 'you're in it, mate!' So funny! And that's how I come to know Barry. You sure you don't want some of this? Anyway, he's on a job in Brixton, but he lives in Wales, so he's to sleeping in his cab, but since we sort of, you know, hit it off and that, he starts stopping over with me, and then he only asks me to move in with him and his kid out in Wales."

"Did you?"

"Well, yeah, man, anything's got to be better than this dump, right? Only it turned out it wasn't."

She wandered off to the toilet, where, above the trickling sound of urine, she continued with her tale.

"Thing is, right, I thought it was gonna be all mountains and sheep and that, but he just had this really like grotty house with really noisy neighbours and that. And no-one was friendly, and they started doing shit that wasn't nice, you know, like, there would be rubbish emptied into our garden, dog mess through the letterbox, you know what I'm saying? Unpleasant! And Barry's son Rhys was so *hostile*, you would not believe it! He hardly never used to say a word to me, man, I was gutted. And Barry was away a lot, and then, one day out of the blue, he only turns around and says to me, 'there's someone else'. Boy what a beating I gave that man! Rhys was so shock him just stand there in silence, I tell you!"

She came back, shaking her head slowly from side to side.

"I gettin' tired now, you can come in with me if you want, but no funny business."

Or a long, cold walk to the squat…

In the wee small hours I became aware of the mattress moving. I peered through half open eyelids. Jacky was lying on her back, with her knees raised, and both hands thrust under the covers. Her head was thrown back, eyes closed, and she was grunting and mumbling as if in dreams.

I slipped quietly out of the bed, into my shoes, glimpsed four A.M. on the alarm clock, and let myself out.

I woke up confused and in pain.

I remembered getting mixed up about which direction home, some strange laughter, shuffling footsteps. And now I was lying in a strange bed feeling like somebody was trying to inflate my brain with a bicycle pump.

I opened my eyes. There was a nurse, smiling at me.

"How are we feelin' this mornin'?" she asked.

I touched my forehead.

"Careful, love, you got a lot of stitches there! What happen to you?"

"I suppose I must have fallen over."

"Well, it look more like you get a beating. You have to go to x-ray."

I swung my legs over the edge of the bed. They hurt too.

"You want me to fetch a porter?"

I stood up and limped a few paces.

"I am a porter."

"Alright, love, whatever you say."

I had to wait an hour at the end of a corridor, but they brought me some Diazepam to ease the aches.

There was an old man with a nose pitted beyond pity, wandering up and down holding what looked like a little grey cardboard hat. Dried blood on his pyjamas.

A harsh voice from the tannoy, "can I have a porter to majors, please, a porter to majors?"

The old man, frightened by the disembodied voice, started muttering to himself, pacing more quickly. His voice grew louder until he was shouting incoherently, thrashing his arms as if beating off a flock of bats. A porter strutted over, upon which the man fell silent, wrapping his arms around his torso like a strait jacket.

I began to feel woozy on the Valium, struggling to recall what had happened after I left the karaoke woman's house. Jacky, that was it. Did we sleep together? Walking home, early morning.

I was sent home with the advice that someone ought to watch over me for a day or two in case I got really sleepy. No evidence of brain damage, apparently. Not since the bruising, anyway.

There wasn't anyone around to watch me. Just the big lazy cat, stretching and rolling over on the mat. I found him something to eat, the smell of which made me retch. I went to bed.

Next morning, Jim was brewing up in the kitchen. He looked round at me and nearly dropped the teapot.

"Oh my God, Billy, what on earth's happened? You look awful. Here, sit down, have a cuppa and tell uncle Jim."

Max came in with a towel round his head, cleaning his teeth.

"Look at poor Billy," said Jim.

Max stopped brushing.

"Oh yes, very Boris Karloff."

He came near to examine.

"Wasn't Declan, was it?"

I started to tell them what I could remember, but Max stopped me when I mentioned the karaoke pub.

"Not the one in Camberwell, near the Maudseley?"

"Yeah. I can't remember the name…"

"Never mind, I know the place. Go on."

"Not much to tell, really. This woman did a song, then I went to her place and…"

Max held up a hand like a traffic cop.

"Please tell me she didn't do 'I will survive'?"

"What's so bad about that?"

"Jacky is. Wacky Jacky."

I glanced at Jim, who shrugged his shoulders.

"And so you went to Jacky's place," continued Max. "And was there, per chance, a man present? Brick shit house, asymmetrical of ear?"

"There wasn't anybody."

"That explains the fact that you can still walk. If he knew you'd been with her, in his house…"

He sat down.

"So, who are they?" asked Jim.

"Regulars," said Max. "She's a fairly harmless la-la who serially picks people up, and he's her psychotic big brother who knocks them down. One presumes he was on his way home, spotted you in the vicinity, and clobbered you just for good measure."

"Sounds like you had a lucky escape," said Jim. "Well, lucky-ish."

Max smiled.

"So, you've encountered Jacky," he said. "Well it's none of my business, chum, but if you were, you know, intimate, I'd advise the clap clinic a.s.a.p."

Lovey dovey

"In my opinion," said Declan, "the 'Laughing Gnome' is vastly underrated."

Jayne laughed.

"If it's not Star Trek it's David bloody Bowie!"

Declan stroked his chin.

"People used to say I looked a bit like him."

"Like the laughing gnome?" said Max.

"Ha, ha, ha."

"Ooh, yes, I can see it now!"

"Very funny. I just happen to think 'Gnome' deserves more regard than it's given."

"You mean it has a subtle allegorical subtext, perhaps?" suggested Max.

"You can stuff your subtext up your arse. It's basically a good pop record."

"Mind you," said Jayne, "you *are* the man who bought 'Mull of Kintyre'."

"Loads of people did."

"Most of them only once though."

"I liked 'Space Oddity'," I said. "A boy played it to me at school on one of those portable cassettes."

"With a toggle control?" asked Declan.

"Yeah. You had to keep your finger on it."

"Left for rewind, right for forward, if I remember rightly. I used to jam mine in place with a pencil. Broke it."

"The machine?"

"The pencil."

"I wanted to hear that song again as soon as it ended," I said.

"Did the boy playing it to you jam a pencil to rewind?" asked Jayne. "Actually, let's pretend I never asked. I can't believe I'm getting drawn into this bloody conversation. I reckon that head injury has turned you soft."

"Mine had a vinyl covered cardboard case, holes punched where the speaker was," said Declan. "And a microphone compartment. I used to hide rolled up pictures from porn mags in it."

Max smiled.

"I hate to think where you kept the microphone."

"I sold it to a lad."

"Who thought you looked like David Bowie, I suppose?"

Jayne stood up.

"Leave it, Max, don't get him started, will you?"

Declan caught hold of her arm.

"Tell my wife I love her very much," he crooned.

She blushed, shrugging him off.

"Don't be so friggin' soft! Anyway we're not married yet. I have to get back to the bar."

"She's got over her flu," I remarked.

"I didn't know she had it," said Declan. "But I'll tell you one thing, flu or no flu, there's no one like her."

Max pretended to vomit.

"Did you see the Blacksmiths Arms?" asked Declan. "Looks to me like someone's tried to torch it."

The pub had been boarded up ever since the incident with the broken window.

"Has anyone seen the owner?" queried Max.

"I think I did, can't be sure," answered Declan. " If it *was* him, he was on crutches."

"My heart bleeds," I said. "I wonder if he'll be back?"

"I don't suppose he'll bother," said Declan. "What's the point, round here? At this rate there'll be no-where left to drink."

"You only ever use the Hope anyway."

"Yeah, but I'm like the married man who flirts. He doesn't go there, but he likes to know he could."

"Imagine these pubs when the docks were alive," mused Max. "An amazing era."

"Yeah," said Declan. "They probably opened early."

I remembered I had got him another Star Trek book, 'Warp Speed and Beyond', from an Oxfam shop. I tossed it over.

"Cheers, Billy! I was getting a bit familiar with the old one."

He started leafing through, concentrating deeply.

Max rolled his eyes.

"And then there were two."

Jayne came back over and prodded Declan until he noticed her.

"Where are you staying tonight?" she asked.

"I'll probably kip at Adam's."

"If that's what you prefer."

"It's like I said, I don't think I should stop at yours' now until after we're married."

Max beamed.

"Ah, isn't he quaint?"

Jayne flushed.

"Shut up, Max, keep out of it will you?"

"Sorry I spoke," he whined, feigning indignation.

"I think I'll get an early night with me new book," said Declan. He gave Jayne a hasty kiss on the cheek and was gone.

"And they say romance is dead," sighed Max, shelling out for more drinks.

"Will you get them yourself?" said Jayne. "On the house."

She dragged a stool close to me, and gently touched the scar on my forehead.

"Right tough guy, you look," she said. "It's healing nicely, though. Amazing how time flies. It's like with the wedding. Seems like one minute he's asking me, the next thing I know we've seen the priest and named the day."

"It's all set, then."

"I've been wanting to tell you. Jesus, it's funny how life is."

"I suppose it is."

"Billy, your poor head. Promise me you'll look after yourself, I hate seeing you hurt."

"Doubles all round," announced Max. "Courtesy of Bob, though he doesn't know it."

"I suppose I'd better give him my notice," said Jayne.

Meanwhile, back at the Throat Nose and Ear, Brian was back.

He pointed at my battered countenance, whistling.

"Christ, Billy, you look like you took a long walk down a short alley!"

"Something like that."

Austin was sloping around again as normal, clearly relieved to have handed back the extra responsibility he had been shouldering. Brenda carried on cursing the job, and Iain talked about his new car.

Brian asked me in to his office later and I sat in front of his desk. He wanted to discuss the supervision session I had with Austin.

"Well, sport," he began, walking round and sitting half-arsed on the edge of his desk. "Old Austin pulled you up, did he?"

"I think so."

He grinned.

"Yeah, know what you mean, not the easiest bloke to read. You did the right thing seeing the M.O. He seems convinced you're under stress due to emotional problems, about which I don't need to know, unless you feel you want to…"

The kettle came to the boil and he made coffee.

"The thing is, mate," he continued, "Austin *was* a bit heavy handed, but you'd be doing yourself a favour if you could just try to play by the rules a bit more."

"I will, thanks."

"No worries. I've had a word with personnel, and there's no need for any further action. Just read this and sign."

He handed me his report, and watching me read, started his characteristic laugh.

"It is a bit rich though, isn't it, being reprimanded for absenteeism by Austin of all people?"

"Well, I wouldn't really call it a reprimand. And he's covered for me when I'm late enough times…"

"Some things I'd better not know! You been down the Prince of Wales at all?"

"We abstained in your honour."

"Well I'm back, so I'll see you there Thursday. And I reckon, to celebrate my triumphal entrance, Brenda and Iain should be there too."

"You pulled it off, then?" I said to Brian, when Thursday came, and we sat at the bar once more.

He raised his eyebrows.

"I think he means getting Bender and Inane to come," explained Austin.

They had just come through the door.

Brenda immediately complained about sitting at the bar.

"I'll find us a nice table," she said.

Away from the bar, Brian was fidgety. He kept arranging and rearranging his money in front of him.

"You shouldn't have it out in full view like that," remarked Brenda. "What if some one gets their hands on it?"

Brian's eye twitched madly.

"Brenda," he said, "I hope you aren't planning to pinch it when I go for a gypsy's?"

She glanced away, sipping her lager and lime.

"I trust we're not harbouring a tea leaf among us?" remarked Iain.

Nobody replied, so he repeated it.

"You are daft," said Brenda.

"Not so green as I'm cabbage looking."

"What's he on about?" Brian whispered.

"Something about cabbages," I said.

"My eldest nephew is a cabbage," said Austin.

Iain started telling us again about his new car.

"It's beautifully fitted out. Stereo radio, lovely mellow sound. And, this'll surprise you, I've only got a telephone in it. Latest thing, portable. Like it says on the box, now I can be in when I'm out!"

"God help us," muttered Brian, getting up to go to the gents.

"Clever geezer who invented that," said Austin.

"Why assume it was a man?" asked Brenda.

"Bound to have been. Women can't invent things. Like they say, if God had meant women to think, he'd have given them a brain."

Brenda pursed her lips.

"If God had had a brain he'd have never invented man in the first place. Anyone for another drink?"

"No you don't," said Iain. "Put your money away, these are on me."

Brenda snapped shut her purse.

Brian helped Iain bring the drinks over.

"Cheers, Iain," he said. "Nice of you to come. You too, Brenda."

"We're glad to see you better," she said. "This'll have to be my last, though, or I'll be tipsy. My Colin's picking me up."

"That's nice," said Iain. "Still driving that Corsair is he?"

He quickly downed his whisky and Canada dry.

"Afraid I must love you and leave you. My mother's corns are very bad. All the best."

Shortly after this we heard the persistent honking of a car hooter. Brenda jumped up and hurried out without finishing her drink.

"Well, Billy, Austin," said Brian, gathering up his money. "Looks like we're down to the hard core. Christ, it's good to be back. I may have had to quit the smokes, but I'll stick to the pub till I drop."

As we moved back to the bar, he flung an arm around each of our shoulders for support.

Max and Jim seemed close. Too close, sometimes.

"I'm going to give it all up for you, Lola, and become your manager," whispered Max one Sunday afternoon. Jim rested his head on Max's shoulder and fluttered his eyelashes.

"Very cosy," I said.

"Cosy fanny tutu," replied Max, sniggering.

Jim gave me a sympathetic smile.

"No Hope today?" he asked.

"Can't, I've got a late shift. I'll have to remain hopeless."

I went Thameside, silty shingle crunching under foot, detritus from centuries of civilisation.

Chris Marlowe. Samuel Pepys. Dickens. Turner. Dors, Diana…

Dense water lapping over them.

A faded coke can bobbed, trapped in a shopping trolley strangled with shredded polythene bags.

Dreary Sunday afternoon.

"Oh, don't start going all Morrissey on me," Liz once said.

Every day, a-ha-ay, is like Sunday.

When the pubs close early.

"You're cool, things're cool," predicted Joo-Lee.

Her house of cards.

Jayne engaged to Declan. I tried to picture him in a topper and tails.

Mourning suit.

"I wouldn't be seen dead in one of them…"

I just keep walking, but the world keeps pace. Inescapable banality of the physical.

My half-there life.
"You ok, Billy?"
It was Peter, on his way to Joe's.
I couldn't answer.
"Here, get yourself a drink."
"I can't take that."
"Go on, spoil yourself! It's not much."
But it was.
"Take care," said Peter.
A solitary gull circled above, crying for company.

"Are you alright?" asked Brenda, yawning and shivering as we started our shift.
"Silly question," she added, before I could answer. "Who's alright when they have to work in this place? Christ, I hate doing lates."
I felt like a tortoise on a cold day, hiding my head.
"Cat got your tongue?" she said.
I thought about the cat at home.
It hardly went out now, and seemed to be getting smellier. Max had tried to evict it, but Jim showed mercy. I realised that it was probably a very old animal.
"You're in a world of your own," said Brenda. "Help me move this patient will you, because I hope you don't think I'm doing it on my own?"
"Why would I think that?"
"I'm sure I don't know why you'd think anything."
"Something the matter?" asked Iain, who had been standing by the window watching someone trying to park their car.
"Brenda wants you to help move Mrs Ryecroft," I told him. "I need coffee."
"Cheek!" exclaimed Brenda. "I like that."
"At last, something you like," I called back.
Mrs Ryecroft followed me.
"I don't need any of you to help move me, thank you," she announced.

Sidestepped a turd and slipped on a banana skin.

Declan confessed to me one evening that he was fooling Jayne about his drinking. He kept an empty three per cent alcohol lager can at home, into which he decanted the very strong stuff he actually consumed.
"I keep the good stuff at the back of the fridge, and every time I go for another beer, I just perform the old swoperoo."
"Why don't you just use a glass?" I asked.
"Psychology, Billy. She sees the weak lager can and it reassures her. She might ask about the contents of a glass, and then I'd be forced to lie."
"So you let a can do your lying for you. And what about the empties, with 'VERY STRONG LAGER' on them?"
He smiled.
"Easily crushed and buried in the bin."
"What if she examines the rubbish?"
"No, Jayne has a trusting nature."
"Even so, she must think it's a bit odd how pissed you get?"
"She puts that down to my condition."
"But why do it?"
"I just don't want her worrying."

"Oh, right. Yes, it must be a great comfort to her to see you getting smashed out of your wits on weak beer."

"What she doesn't know won't hurt her. Anyway, not long now before she makes an honest man of me."

The shifts at the hospital seemed to be ganging up on me.

We all got by, somehow, by taking slightly desperate unofficial breaks, be they coffee, fag, or both.

None of us seemed to have much in common to talk about, but Austin was always good value.

On one sleety afternoon, as I hudddled with him and Brian in a doorway out the back, he returned to his experience with photography.

"I was assigned to take shots during the Falklands war," he remarked, tapping ash from his cigarette with a long, burnished nail.

"I'd have pictured you at the front, taking pot shots," said Brian.

"I was, man. You any idea how dangerous photojournalism is?"

"I'm sure some of your pictures were highly dangerous."

"You taking the piss?"

"Is that a telephoto lens in your pocket…?"

"Yeah, yeah, so easy to mock."

"From crackpot to snapshot."

"If you knew, you wouldn't joke about it."

"Rough shoot, was it?"

"You don't want to know, man, you do not want to know!"

He stubbed his fag and trotted off to the wards.

"He's right there," said Brian. "I bloody don't! I sometimes wonder if he's breathing the same air as the rest of us, know what I mean?"

He lit a cigarette, casting me a guilty glance.

"Just the odd one," he said.

He was finished. In fact his shift had ended half an hour before, but he often lingered after work for a chat.

I was due to meet a new patient, a wheelchair user who needed helping to a ward, so I went to it.

The new arrival was a young French woman, wearing a sort of gauze mask over her mouth, and dark glasses. She kept uttering slightly muffled expressions of discontent. *"Putain! Merde! Oh, je le crois pas! C'est dur, c'est trop…"*

I decided it might be best not to try my pigeon French on her. She didn't seem particularly inclined to conversation. But when I delivered her to her bedside, and turned to go, she said, in perfect R.P.

"Thank you for not having bothered me with small talk. I cannot tell you how much that means."

She went straight in at number three in my 'wonder what happened to' chart.

Dropping to number four, Joe's uncle Mike. Still at number two, the Maitresse. And, for the ninth consecutive week, at number one, it's Liz.

The rest of my shift was entirely routine. I was beginning to wonder how long I could carry on. I couldn't imagine pushing trolleys until I was sixty-five. But what else? Drumming was taking me nowhere. Maybe I was destined for eternal factotumry.

Max found it irritating when I said such things.

"You should be grateful you've got a job, there are millions of unemployed."

It was like being reminded, as a child, of those starving in Africa. It didn't improve my appetite.

"William, are you with us?"

It was Brenda, tapping my arm.

"Come on, you're supposed to be helping me with Mr Chatfield."

Marvellous! Mr Chatfield, though uncertified, was undoubtedly the maddest patient in the building.

Brenda frowned.

"Talk about day dreaming. I don't think you can be getting enough sleep."

"Sorry. Mr C on safari again?"

"If, by 'on safari', you mean rampaging around the building knocking things over, then the answer's yes. Listen, that's him laughing. You keep these doors covered, and I'll flush him out. Make sure he doesn't get past you."

Within minutes he was dashing towards me, red faced, trilling with laughter. Spotting me, he slowed down, and eyed me, head cocked, for an instant, before making a sudden grab for a fire extinguisher. I managed to get hold of his arms before he could reach it, but he kicked me on the shins and struggled free.

"You're letting him get away," shouted Brenda, out of breath.

He was already half way down the corridor before I realised I was holding his pyjama top. Now he was discarding the bottoms.

"Oh, that's all I need," said Brenda. "Why did you have to encourage him?"

We set off after him, and eventually backed him into a corner, where he became submissive.

"I'm naughty," he said, panting.

"Nutty, more like," murmured Brenda.

We persuaded him to get dressed and Brenda sat him by his bed with a pair of headphones so he could listen to the radio.

"Once he's got those on, he usually stays put," she said. "I don't know about you, but that's tired me out. We'll sleep sound tonight."

I dreamed I was at a rock festival in a field of mud painted green. The affair was fizzling out as the wan dawn arrived, and Liz was strumming a guitar on stage, singing a mawkish soul song. Her audience was comprised mostly of people assigned to clear litter, but the bar was still open and I was at it, sipping a half of flat Guinness. Jayne was cleaning glasses, but she didn't recognise me. Declan appeared, dancing with Joo-Lee, except it was Max dressed in her clothes.

I woke earlier than usual, wanting Guinness, but I settled for tea.

Jim came into the kitchen.

"Hello dear, I didn't know you were here," he said, scratching the backs of his legs.

"No Max?" I asked.

"In bed, sulking. We had a bit of a tiff about me doing Lola."

"I thought he loved it."

"So did I. I think what he doesn't love is the attention he seems to think I'm getting."

"Bit possessive?"

"Le mot juste, Billy. Want some toast?"

We chewed it over.

"I suppose the honeymoon period's over," said Jim. "Max has been a bit…Oh, I don't know, hark at me! At least he's there."

I could hear Liz crooning plaintively.

Jim regarded me, automatically buttering more toast.

"Billy, I know you're not exactly Sir Laughalot, but you look a tinsy bit extra down in the mouth to me. Something up?"

"Oh, not really. It just seems like everyone's either getting themselves together, or going to pieces."

"You're doing all right though, got your job."

"Yeah, it's ok. It's just…well, it's not what I thought it was going to be like when I came down to London."

"What *did* you expect?"

"Oh, you know, streets paved with gold discs, diamond studded flunkies…"

"Slow down, you're losing me."

"Oh, you know. Flights of fancy."

"Sounds like my kind of airline! I'll be the stewardess and you can be the captain."

"You see, that's my problem. I could talk like this for hours."

"Daydream believer?"

"You said it. I'm due in at work in less than an hour, and the thought of it doesn't thrill me at all."

"Not at all?"

The morning sun illuminated every crumb on the table.

"Not a jot."

"Well skip it then! Skive, and we'll go for a walk. It's much too nice to be in."

"I shouldn't…"

"Billy, there are so many things we tell ourselves we shouldn't do. And then we spend our old age wondering why the hell we never did 'em. Look how long it's taken me to get my arse on stage. I was wearing frocks when I was three! I'm nearly forty now, a washed up old queen having a last stab at stardom. I know it'll fizzle out, but I'm squeezing sparks out of it while I can."

"Where are we walking?"

"That's better. How about the farm?"

"That might be quite a long walk."

"No, you know, the City farm. Honestly, Billy, it's twenty minutes away and you've never been."

Surrey docks. The slightly salty air was tinged with the whiff of manure.

"I've always loved animals," said Jim. "Been out with a few an' all."

A goat stared at us, oblong pupils in grey-green eyes. Jim started to laugh.

"You know what? He looks just like Max does when he's got a cob on."

"No need to insult the beast."

"Billy, you are very naughty. Oh look, over there, look at those geese! Women's Institute or what?"

"I think they heard you."

They were rushing towards us, necks extended.

"Oh blimey," said Jim. "It's me they want. Ow! Get off!"

He laughed and hopped as they pecked at his calves.

Jim and me in the City farm, Max and Joo-Lee in the funny one.

We walked back along the river, Limehouse reach, and I suggested a pint in the Hope. Jim looked thoughtful.

"Oh, all right. But I'll just have a half."

Bob was just ringing last orders.

"Start drinking up now, please," he shouted. "I've got a life outside of here even if you haven't."

He handed us our drinks.

"Make it snappy, will you?"

We rushed them, and were soon back on the sunny street. I had the taste now, and fancied another.

"We should be able to get some cans somewhere."

Jim didn't seem keen.

"Why don't we have a bit of lunch, my treat?"

"Trying to steer me off the beer?"

He smiled.

"I wouldn't tell you what to do."

I wanted wayward company, Joo-Lee with her insouciant smile. But her carefree days were mothballed.

"Another time," said Jim. "I have to be off soon anyway, gig tonight. I'm opening for Su Pollard."

Back home, he started getting ready. I went upstairs, sat on the bed and stared at my drum kit.

Cupboard love

Brian had his back to me when I entered his office, looking out of the window. His shoulders were shaking. Sensing my approach, he turned.

"She cracks me up," he said, pointing outside to where Brenda was hurrying along the pavement. "Always the same bloody coat, rain or shine, always talking to herself. Cursing the job, probably. Always on time though. She did a double shift yesterday, mate."

This was his way of broaching the subject of my unplanned absence.

"Sorry about that. All the 'phone boxes round our way are out of order."

"Out of order," he repeated. "Yeah. Well, listen, you'd better put something in writing. Better still, I reckon you better take it as emergency leave. I think that looks better."

He scratched the hair on his neck, and eased a buttock onto the corner of his desk. Having to admonish me, even so leniently, didn't come easy.

"Bloody stuffy in here," he remarked.

Brenda bustled in, coat folded neatly over her arm, and looked at us in turn.

"Hello William," she said. "Nice of you to grace us with your presence. I could say more, but right now I have to go and relieve Iain."

"Forget it, mate," said Brian, as the door closed on her. "She's glad of the overtime. You haven't heard this from me, but her old man's crook with a slipped disk. Self-employed, no medical insurance. And the good news is, you're on shift with her. Now."

"Thanks for yesterday, Brenda," I said, catching up.

"Yes, well, don't make a habit of it."

As we arrived at the ward, Iain, coming off shift, immediately presented us with a prone patient in bed with a sheet drawn over his head.

"Bloody great," hissed Brenda. "Get a trolley."

I obeyed, while she went round to the other side of the bed.

"You'll have to help me, Iain, don't go wandering off just yet."

"Your servant," he replied.

As Brenda started to gently ease her hands under the body, the sheet suddenly shot back to reveal the grinning face of Austin.

At first she hardly reacted. Her mouth opened, but no words came. Then her face grew pink, lips quivering and tightening, until, with a ripping shriek of frustration she began repeatedly pummelling Austin about the head with her elbows.

"Stupid, stupid!" she cried.

She turned her head and strode off in the direction of Brian's office.

"I told you it wasn't a good idea," remarked Iain.

"Maybe so," said Austin, "but that don't give her the right to beat up on me. What a bitch! That was assault man, and I'm reporting her."

"That would also, in my opinion, not be a particularly good plan," said Iain. "And perhaps you'd better get out of that bed before the ward round arrives."

As he turned to leave, Brenda came stomping back. She gave him a dirty look.

"I trust you had nothing to do with this?"

Iain kept walking as if he hadn't heard.

Austin, sitting up, flinched as she bent to his level.

"As for you," she said, "I've decided not to take it any further. Your sort aren't worth it. Now, if you'll let William and I get on with our work."

As Austin sauntered off, we could just make out the sound of him singing, "trouble double double" under his breath.

Brenda shook her head.

"I actually think he's mentally subnormal. Either that or he's on hash."

We managed to cooperate with one another quite well for the rest of the shift, and Brenda was unusually affable as we knocked off.

"Any plans for the afternoon?" she asked.

"I never seem to plan anything really."

"I might see a film," she said. "There's that 'Passage to India' at our local. Do you like films?"

I hesitated, fighting the urge to recommend 'Thundercrack'.

"Well, enjoy yourself whatever you do. I'll see you tomorrow."

She gave a little wave over her shoulder, just a flutter of fingers.

I went to retrieve my jacket from Brian's office. There was no response to my knock, so I went in. Brian was sitting at his desk, head slumped forward on his chest. I went closer, listened for a moment to his light snoring, quietly lifted my jacket and left.

I had some shopping in my locker, and was on my way back from fetching it when I heard a sound coming from one of the storerooms. It grew louder as I walked down the dark corridor, a monotonous, guttural noise like someone repeating the word 'wharf.'

The door of the room was ajar.

As my eyes adjusted, I made out the figure of a person. It was Iain, and the sounds were coming from him.

He had his back to me, and his trousers were round his ankles, red briefs stretched across the underside of his buttocks.

Just visible over his shoulder, a face, eyes screwed shut in an expression redolent equally of agony and ecstasy.

Brenda.

He doesn't smoke the same cigarettes as me

Jayne was serving.

"My last week in this dump," she reminded me. "I'll miss it though. And you."

She told me Bob had been trying to sell up, but there hadn't been any takers.

"They may as well sell it after you've gone," I said.

"Ah! Won't be the same without me, eh?"

She pulled me a free one.

Declan was hunched over his book, occasionally reacting out loud to the story.

"Like fuck you could!...Sound!...Bollocks!"

"He's easily pleased, bless him," remarked Jayne. "But he's an idiot with the drinking. He's only been sneaking Special Brews at home and badly hiding the empties."

"He doesn't know you know?"

"I know. I mean, no, yeah, we'll have to have it out. People do worse."

Max wobbled in.

"What a shit of a day!" he slurred. "Set 'em up Jayne, babes, 'cause a thirsty man is'n angry man."

"Plastered," said Jayne.

Max leaned towards her, squinting.

"So what? I may've had one or two to wind down. Let she who's without gin cast the firsh-tone."

"I never touch the stuff, but I'm sure you'll get plenty stoned anyway."

She mixed him a double.

"You're 'n angel, gimme."

He swallowed half of it.

"Oh yes, yes. Def'nitely getting a halo."

"Work getting to you?" I asked.

"Ah, the lov'ly Billy. What-a-you think?"

"I think you're having visions."

"Double visions, darling. Behold, our Lady Jayne with the burning bush."

"Just remember, it's not burning for you," said Declan, looking up from his book.

"Steady on the two of you," said Jayne. "You're neither of you too big for a hiding."

"Promises," said Max. "They tease me, Billy. Talk to me."

"Ok. This may not be the best time to ask, but how's Joo-Lee?"

Max pinched my cheek.

'Ah, the divine Ms Rothman. Well, despite the best efforts of her shrink, I think she's mending."

"Are the shrinks no good?" asked Declan.

"Listen, old fruit, they're a bunch of fucking mountebanks. If anyone can unrevel, un*ravel* the knots in that girl's mind, it is I, Maximilian Subotsky, the one and only."

"There couldn't be any more of you," said Declan. "That would just be cruel."

'Don't try to be clever, spud-lover. You want a drink, I suppose."

'Does the Pope freshen up in the woods?"

'God, how I'm going to miss your little witticisms! Set 'em up again, Jayne, and one for yourself."

'So you reckon she'll be all right?" I asked.

"J Rothman? I think she's about ready for the world. That's what I'll be pushing for anyway. Enough about work already! Declan, you rascal, what're you doing about your stag night?"

"Haven't thought about it."

"Listen to it! 'Haven't thought about it.' D'you ever think about anything?"

"Loads o' things."

"Such as?"

"I dunno. Brick laying."

"Marvellous! And is that what's on your mind right now, laying a brick?"

"No, right now what's on my mind is how can I murder a patronising homosexual without fear of detection."

"Ha ha."

"Anyway, what's the point of a stag do?"

"You get drunk with your mates."

"I don't have any mates."

"That smarts. D'you hear him, Billy? Says he hasn't got any mates."

"You know what I mean. Look, I don't see the point of doing what I do every night and calling it a stag do."

Max sighed.

"I wish I'd never asked. Hey, Jayne, how about you and me having a hen night? Sod 'em!"

"Maybe, Max."

"Don't wet yourself, will you?"

Later, as we walked home, Max leaned on me heavily, and when we got in, slumped onto the living room mattress.

The serving hatch shot open to reveal Jim, po-faced.

Max pointed, sniggering.

"It's like being on the Enterprise. We have visual contact."

Jim tutted.

"Just wait till you come back down to earth. Dinner's spoiled."

He shut the hatch.

Max was nodding.

"We're losing contact, Jim," he mumbled.

It was handover time at the hospital.

"I've got work as a hand model," announced Austin, surveying with raised eyebrows the condition of his fingernails.

"Let's hear it," said Brian, twitchy eyed.

"Simple, man, piece of piss. They do these close ups, right, of me wearing a ring, or a watch or something, for catalogues and stuff, know what I mean? I tell you, my hands are in big demand."

"You'd better get them insured," remarked Brenda.

"Yes," added Brian, "they could easily get damaged working here."

"I use gloves, man, health and safety."

"Well fetch a pair, we've dirty work to do," said Brenda.

As they got up to go, Brian squeezed Austin's arm.

"Listen, mate, be sure to give me fair notice when you need time off for another hand job."

Austin shrugged him off.

Iain was off work with a 'stress related illness', and there was a new woman standing in. Her name was Beryl, small, but very wide around the waist. Her short legs tapered down to very small feet that were forced into even smaller shoes, pointed, with spindly high heels. She had a loud, deep-throated laugh that obviously irritated Brenda. In fact, since the departure of Iain, there wasn't much that didn't.

"That fucking woman," she hissed, hearing the guffaw. "What's she got to laugh about?"

"Maybe she thinks jokes?" I suggested.

"She is a joke. Have you seen the size of her? You have to breathe in when she passes you in the corridor."

"She's all right."

"She's a weeble."

I asked Brian to put me on shifts with Beryl or Austin whenever possible. Brenda's raised irascibility was hard to take, especially when accompanied by the recurring image of her grimacing mug in the broom cupboard.

Winter was bowing out, leaves starting to appear, and the day of Jayne and Declan's departure was imminent. My time slogging at the hospital was divided with slumming in the Hope.

I was walking home down Rotherhithe Street, when the yellow-grey of storm clouds gathered, and the first big drops began to hit, randomly dappling the pavement, the parched flagstones throwing up the aroma of dampened dust.

Several dogs, disturbed by a rumble of thunder, began barking, the sound echoing around the stairwells of Lavender House.

I passed a wrecked ambulance, with ripped, tie-dye curtains, overrun with cats.

Rubbish, no longer collected, was piling up around the bins. On the dingy concrete stairs, a discarded syringe cracked under my shoe.

This really wouldn't do, must get myself a little *pied a terre.*

I retraced my steps and headed for the Hope.

A dog, sitting at Declan's feet, scratched itself behind the ear with a hind leg, and gave a strangled yawn almost like a yodel.

Declan shifted his feet under scrutiny from Jayne.

"What in God's name is that?" she asked, leaning over the bar.

"It's a dog."

"You don't say! Whose dog?"

Declan lowered his eyes.

"I've sort of adopted her."

"And how're we supposed to take *her* with us t'Ireland, may I ask?"

"I dunno. In a basket, maybe."

Max smiled.

"Pub grub, mongrel in a basket."

Jayne raised an eyebrow at me.

"Is the whole frigging world losing its marbles?"

"Either that or we are."

"God have mercy! I mean, you couldn't make it up."

Max burbled something about his supper, and walked diagonally out the door.

"It's a sorry state when it's you and me the only ones sort of sane," remarked Jayne.

"You and me against the world."

"Billy, don't be a hero," she smirked.

"I wouldn't know where to start."

"I've named her Theresa," said Declan.

Iain came back to work on 'light duties'.

"That means he's not really up to the job," confided Brian. "The union rep. will have found a loophole, Billy, believe you me. Take Austin. It's a badge of honour with him to have survived so many disciplinaries. You better grab your lunch, mate, time marches on."

Iain looked up from his Daily Mail as I joined him.

"Oh, it's you."

"Seemingly."

"Very droll."

He started to prise open the lid of a Tupperware box.

"Incidentally," he said, eyes on the lunchbox, "is anything up with Brenda?"

"Like what?"

"I don't know. She just seems a bit off with me. Wonder what's got into her?"

I concentrated on the embroidered golf clubs motif on his green polo shirt.

"She's fed up with it," I said.

"What?"

"Everything."

"Oh."

Austin broke the silver on a Kit Kat, dropping the wrapper on the table. It said '10,000 £5 notes to be instantly won!'

Iain flipped it over.

"Story of my life. Better luck next time."

The sound of Beryl's laugh echoed down the corridor.

"I don't see why they keep her on," remarked Iain.

"It's to make up for you," answered Austin.

Iain snapped the lid on his lunchbox and walked out.

Gueule

Despite my unplanned absences from work, I was still entitled to some leave. Recalling Joo-Lee's Paris honeymoon plan, I decided I would go solo. I could just about afford a short trip, if I was frugal with the francs.

Victoria coach station was choked with exhaust fumes and irritable travellers. People kept trying to edge forward before their coach arrived

"This queuing system was clearly devised by chimpanzees," remarked a woman pulling a suitcase on wheels.

A man wearing a leather pork pie hat nodded.

"Sounds like they're doing the announcements an' all."

By chance I found the Paris charabanc chugging over in the bay intended for Glasgow.

The French driver waited for everyone to settle, then stood in the aisle and made the following announcement.

"Attention, please, you are not to be smoking, eating or drinking on this vehicle. No bottle, can or chip packet, no wrapper. This is my bus, and I have to clean it. Thank you."

He climbed into his cockpit, and people exchanged glances like subversive school kids.

"Wow!" said the woman next to me, with a French accent. She had a lot of dark curly hair, and looked about twenty. There was a cardboard box on her knees, and I wondered if it contained a packed lunch, and, if so, would she have the nerve to eat any of it.

I slipped a quarter bottle of Captain Morgan's from my pocket, and quietly twisted the cap. The woman sitting in front of me turned her head to look. She was wearing a straw hat with a fake sunflower attached, and every time I opened the bottle, the hat would turn. You could almost hear her neck creak. Eventually I raised the bottle to her, and she quickly pretended to be asleep.

The girl beside me smiled, holding her box with care.

"Lunch?" I asked.

"Locusts," she answered.

There were faint scuffling sounds from the box.

"Is part of an exposition," she explained. "You know, installation. We have this glass case full up of wheat straws, and all these locusts in there. Some have died, so I bring more. Bigs one!"

"Big ones?"

"Yes."

The driver suddenly turned off all the lights, and my companion soon nodded off. Next morning, as we got off at the grubby station, she handed me a flyer.

"Why don't you come see the expo?"

I wanted to hint that I had nowhere to stay, and rode the Métro with her until she got up at Le Kremlin Bicetre.

"See you, maybe?" she said.

I stayed on, and she gave a little wave as the train rumbled past.

There was a small dry stain on the shoulder of my jacket where she had slept against me on the night coach.

I stepped out into the dusty sunny air at Place de la Concorde, and went walking towards Montmartre. I wanted a look at the Sacre-Coeur. First, though, some breakfast. I found a nice, dark little back street bar, and ordered coffee, pain au chocolat and a red wine.

A transvestite sitting at a table near the door raised his glass. He was an old man, with beautiful make-up and a pretty grey dress, conversing with anyone who would listen, and cursing those who wouldn't. He told me he was eighty-six, and had had as many lovers.

"Un pour chaque année, mais, pour la plupart quand j'étais jeune. Jeune comme toi!"

I didn't feel particularly jeune, but his smile, and the wine, bucked me up a tad.

"Salut, mon cher," he called, as I sauntered out into the pale sunshine. "Bonne chance!"

As I ascended the narrow steps to the rear of the Sacre-Coeur, the pale building loomed, and beyond it spread the wide view of the city.

There were 'Keep off the Grass' signs.

I bought a little bottle of brandy in one of the few grocery stores, and as I walked, taking a sip, someone stared. I felt like a wino.

If Joo-Lee were with me I wouldn't have cared.

I was still wandering aimlessly as evening began to fall. I walked in the shadow of a long wall surrounding a building called the 'Hôpital des Invalides'.

It reminded me of Maidstone prison. Kent, where I grew up. The orchards and narrow lanes. Walking the dog and talking to myself.

I dodged into a P.M.U. bar and stood on failed betting slips drinking a demi. The patron shot glances at me as if irritated to have a tourist stand at the bar. Or perhaps he was just tired. Certainly, he yawned a lot. Then he started putting chairs on tables and sweeping up.

I went out and found a park to doss in.

Under globe lamps on iron posts were huddled a few tramps, murmuring and swearing. A bottle rolled. Vin de table, but no table.

There was a vacant bench in a darker spot, so I got my sleeping bag from my rucksack, stuffed my money and passport down my pants, and tried to settle.

I was roused early from a patchy sleep by a shrill voice.

"Fifi, pas ici! Fifi, viens!"

A woman in a long overcoat and high-heeled, patent leather shoes was calling an enormous white poodle with a pink ribbon on its head. Fifi looked self consciously around, arched her back and had a long, shuddering shit.

I sat up, shivering. The grass all around was white with dew, and there was mist hanging around the railings.

My stomach felt empty, but I had no appetite.

"Christ," I said aloud, "I think I'm squat-sick."

I found in my pocket the flyer given to me by the girl on the coach.

"Expo. des Arts Etonnants."

It wasn't far, so I decided I might as well go and see those locusts in action.

At the entrance were two men painted head to toe, hanging up in matching frames. For a long time they remained perfectly still, then one of them suddenly grabbed a small girl by the arm.

She started to cry.

I found the locusts on the ears of corn. They didn't move much either, nor did they grab me.

So far so un-astonished.

At the end of a corridor there was a little alcove with a grass floor. In fact it was completely covered in grass, including a small bench. I stepped in, sat down, and got out my little bottle of cheap cognac.

Immediately I was joined by a woman of about sixty, with reddish, pitted face, sere grey hair and chin stubble. She gestured for the bottle, spun the cap and took a swig. I gave her a smile and a nod, and she said something I didn't understand, laughed, stroked my cheek and ran off with the drink.

I stuck my head out, but there was no sign of her. Coming down the corridor, though, was the girl from the coach.

I stood up as she came towards me.

"Salut!" she called. "I'm Rahma, I was next you on the bus."

"How're you doing?"

"I am doing all right. Hey, I didn't get your name."

"Billy."

"Ok, Billy. Sorry about this woman, she, you know..."

She made a motion with her hand as if raising a glass to her lips.

"I shouldn't have got that bottle out."

"Ca va. You fancy to have a drink now? I know a nice bar."

She led me to the exit, where a small crowd was gathered outside, looking up at something behind us and smiling. It was a big screen showing video images of the show.

I thought I spotted the old roué, dancing about in front of some Japanese tourists. Rahma took my arm.

"Allez, I want to show you my favourite bar."

It was called 'Le Rat qui Rit', and above the door was a painting of that blithe rodent wearing a beret and shades.

Rahma got herself a coke, and a beer for me. She smiled at me over her glass as if she found me amusing.

"I saw your locusts," I said.

"You like it? I hope they didn't bother you too much on the bus. And I want to say sorry for going asleep on you."

"It's ok."

"It's embarrassing."

She had small, neat hands, short nails.

"It's nice."

She gave me a wide smile, a gold tooth shining.

"You think so?"

Her expression suddenly changed.

"Oh, merde!" she uttered, looking beyond me towards the entrance.

I turned, and there, hastening towards us, was the old bottle-snatcher. She was still clutching it, making straight for our table. Rahma was shaking her head, gesturing for the woman to go away, but she just grinned and kept coming.

Arriving at her table, she immediately kissed Rahma twice on both cheeks.

"Salut, ma soeur!" she said, sitting down.

Rahma said nothing.

The woman put the bottle in front of me.

"I give you it back," she said.

She pulled a handkerchief from her sleeve and started wiping her face with it.

Rahma sighed.

"Billy, meet Fawzi. My brother."

He laughed, pulling off the grey wig to reveal dark, tightly curled hair.

"Ca va?" he said. "I hope you don't mind the joke."

"I didn't want him to get you, Billy, really," said Rahma. "I'm sorry. I fucked up, right?"

"It's ok," I said. "Anyway he brought the bottle back."

"Voila, c'est cool," said Fawzi.

He ordered a round, and his pleated skirt and angora cardigan didn't seem to perturb the waiter at all.

"They know me here. I'm celebrated!"

"He's crazy," said Rahma. "The Travis Bickle of Paris."

"I drive taxi at night," explained Fawzi.

Rahma touched my hand.

"Hey, why don't you come to my place and let me make you something to eat?"

Fawzi drove us to her little suburban flat, and got cleaned up and changed while Rahma started getting busy in the kitchen.

"I have to go work," said Fawzi. "Actually, where are you staying, Billy?"

"Haven't really decided."

He looked at my beaten up old rucksack.

"You know what, why don't you stay here?"
Rahma came out from the kitchen
"Fawzi, qu'est-ce que tu fais?"
"Quoi? Quoi?"
"C'est pas a toi de l'inviter!"
"Oh, Rahma, c'est pas grave."
"Ta gueule, Fawzi!"
She turned to me.
"Sorry about him, he's so fucking crazy in his head."
He laughed.
"Ok, I can drop you at my place. C'est dommage, quand-meme. You will miss the food. She is useless, but she makes nice couscous."
"It's ok," said Rahma. "You can stay if you want."
Fawzi jingled his car keys.
"Well, I leave you, salut mon ami, salut ma soeur!"
Rahma got me to open a bottle of wine while she put food on plates.
"I hope you not pissed off at me?" she said.
"Why?"
"I think maybe I put you in a corner."
"It's a pretty nice one, as corners go."
Later, as we sat on the sofa, she fell asleep on my shoulder for the second time. I watched her for a while, her lips slightly parted in slumber.

I woke face down on a cushion that reeked of tobacco and stale wine. There was also the aroma of fresh coffee.
"Bonjour!" called Rahma, coming in with two white cups. She was wearing just a baggy T-shirt with 'I love Snoopy' on it, and looked beautiful, with her pale face, dark eyes, and uncombed hair. She sat on the arm of the couch, swinging a bare foot, and lit a Marlboro. For a second, she might have been Joo-Lee.
"What are you thinking of?" she asked.
Joo-Lee would have known.
"Too many things," I said.
"I have to go to the Expo."
"I have to catch the coach."
"A Londres?"
I nodded, and she came over and kissed me on the cheek, and then on the mouth.
"Bye," she said quietly.
"Bye."
I picked up my rucksack.
"Rahma?"
"Oui?"
"Look after the locusts."

Ding dong

I had to travel overnight again due to cancelled coaches. The man next to me, wearing a shiny blue shirt with sweat patches, went to sleep on my shoulder. Waking, he made a great fuss of sorting out his newspaper.
I arrived in Victoria coach station feeling grubby and tired, and was now due on shift in two hours. Just enough time to tube home, change and shave.

There were no razors.

I hammered irritably on Max's door, and it swung open. Jim was getting up to answer, covering himself with a sheet. He was alone.

"Nice break?" he asked, fumbling for his underpants.

"Sorry for bursting in. I wanted Max's razor."

"Over there. Don't tell him I let you have it whatever you do. Very possessive he is. Coffee?"

I had a quick one, and just made work on time on a bike that Jim said had 'turned up' in the flat. It had a lot of gears, and I whizzed over Blackfriars Bridge, the breeze off the river in my face. I was tempted to hop off and find a beer, watch the people bustle, but duty called and duty won.

As I locked up the bike outside the hospital, I realised it was Joo-Lee's.

I was mulling this over as I went on shift with Brenda.

"Bonjour!" she said, minty bright.

"You've changed your lip-stick," I remarked.

She flushed.

"Suits you, too."

"Thank you, William."

"De rien. How's it been?"

"Oh, same old same old, you know. Beryl's gone though, now that Iain's back on top of things."

She strode purposefully ahead.

Austin came from the other direction, repeatedly bouncing a squash ball off the wall and catching it, smack, neatly in his palm.

"Vive la Revolution!" he shouted.

Everyone was being amusing.

By lunchtime I was starting to nod.

"Are we keeping you up?" remarked Iain.

"Yes," I told him, "you are."

"Oh dear, left Monsieur sense de humour abroad have we?"

"Frenchmen are supposed to be so fucking macho, so Latin lover and all that shit," ranted Declan. "They're nothing but little runty guys who stink of garlic and suck each other's knobs in the men's bogs."

"Not all bad then," observed Max.

"I'm going to miss your cultural observations, Declan," I said. "Maybe you could record me some on tape so I can play them back after you've gone."

"I told you, I sold my tape recorder."

He had been one of those youths who sold everything, a boy merchant, trading in electrical goods, football cards, information, cigarettes and dirty magazines.

I was the opposite, a lad who looked after his toys. 'Action Man', in my hands, had spent most of his time sitting at a cardboard desk in a shoebox office. 'Admin Man.'

"After I learn how, I'll write you," promised Declan.

"If I'm still here."

"You thinking of moving?"

"Declan, dear," said Max, "just because you and Jayne are about to peregrinate, it doesn't necessarily follow that young Billsome should be upping sticks."

"Shut up, I wasn't asking you. Are you, Billy?"

"Maybe."

"What about our hen night, Max?" asked Jayne. "How about tomorrow?"

"Chill the champagne, love, and arrange for Declan not to be here."

"Why should I be turfed out on me last night? I've more of less kept this place solvent."

Max scoffed,

"We all know about you and solvents. You can do something with Billy."

"What about it?" he asked.

"Well, tomorrow's Thursday. You could always meet me after work, and we'll have a few in the pub near the hospital."

I told him about the Prince of Wales nights.

"I suppose," he replied.

"What's this mate of yours like then?" asked Brian, puffing on a cigarette in the doorway. Rain dripped around us, and steam floated up from my coffee.

"I look forward to these cosy breaks," I said.

"Bit of a nutter, right? Must be if he's getting hitched. Don't worry, we'll give him a send off."

Later, as Brian, Austin and I ambled out, we found Declan hanging around in the rain. He had his hands in his pockets, shoulders hunched in a futile attempt to improve the shelter provided by his too-small, quilted anorak. He raised a thin hand in greeting, and I introduced him.

Brian patted him on the back.

"So this is your last night of freedom, eh?"

"Nearly," said Declan, his voice quieter than usual.

We settled at the bar, and Brian got in a round of beers with shorts. Declan knocked his shot back and chased it with a long swallow of lager.

"I hear you're going back to Ireland?" remarked Austin.

"Yeah."

"Which part?"

"Drogheda."

"No, I mean North or South."

"Well, South."

"Not the British bit?"

Declan smiled and drank the rest of his pint.

"No. The Irish bit. Anyone for any more?"

He pulled a damp, crumpled tenner from his pocket.

"Beaut!" said Brian. "So, what are you planning to do when you get home?"

"I dunno. There's not a lot to do. Me Dad's a mechanic so I might help him a bit."

"You know about motors?" asked Austin, examining the head on his Guinness.

"A bit."

"I was going to be in the Royal Engineers."

"What happened?"

"What do you mean?"

"Well, what stopped you?"

Austin took a slow sip of stout.

"You wouldn't want to know."

"Try me."

"Not this time."

"Oh well, you're probably best out of it."

"What do you mean?"

"Doesn't matter."

"You ever been to Belfast?"

"Only on a day trip. Bit of sightseeing. We did Newry on the way home."

Austin looked at me.

"Is he trying to be funny?"

"He wouldn't know how, would you Declan?" I replied.

Brian rubbed his hands together.

"Come on lads, drink up! This poor sod's soon to be spliced, it's the least we can do to send him off with a hangover."

"My round," said Austin.

He got himself a half this time.

"I sometimes think about going back home," said Brian. "Must be missing the sheep. No, seriously, I haven't got anything to draw me back. All my folks are dead, and I'm pretty well settled here."

"I could be called anywhere at any time," said Austin.

"What, for some hand modelling?" I asked.

"To areas of conflict," continued Austin. "Know what I mean?"

"Don't tell me," said Declan. "You're a diplomat."

"Diplomacy won't sort out the trouble your people have stirred up."

"My people? I don't have any people."

"You know what I mean. The troubles. You can't hide from it."

Declan laughed.

"Well if that isn't a case of the pot calling the kettle black! You should look in your own back yard."

"My back yard is Plumstead. We do the right thing."

"Sure. Muggers, drug dealers, England's finest."

Austin moved his glass away from him, and prodded an index finger against Declan's pigeon chest.

"Seeing as you're obviously a shilling short, I'm gonna pretend I didn't hear that. Now, drink up."

"Delighted," answered Declan. He opened his throat, sank the remaining three-quarters of his pint, gulped his whisky, and slipped down from his stool.

"It's been nice," he declared, "but I think I'll go check up on Max and Jayne."

He shook Brian's hand,

"Nice meeting you. Cheerio Billy. Oh, and *you*," he swung a sudden left which cracked Austin above his right eye, splitting the eyebrow.

Checking the wound, and seeing blood on his fingers, Austin stood up.

"You just made a bad mistake," he said, grasping the front of Declan's shirt, and pulling him near.

"A...very...bad...mistake!" he reiterated, punctuating his words with slaps to Declan's face.

Declan touched his hot cheeks, shook his head and smiled.

"Well, I suppose that makes us even. Normally, of course, I'd deck you anyway, but I've a fiancée waiting, so why waste me time?"

I caught up with him later in the Hope.

He was dancing with Max to 'Every Breath You Take.'

Jayne smiled at me.

"Did you spike his drink or something? Look at the two of them. I hope he's not marrying the wrong girl!"

"So do I."

"Come here Billy."

She put her arms round me and held on so I could hardly breathe.

"By the way," she said, letting go, and picking at my sleeve. "Declan's got a spot of blood on him. Don't tell me there was trouble?"

"What's he said?"

"That makes sense? Very little."

"He was provoked."

"I knew it! And would you look at him now? You'd never think he could hurt a fly."

His head was supported on Max's chest, as they falteringly circled, arm in arm.

"Wish I had a camera," she said. "Come on, Billy, those two are totally out of it. It's you and me."

She got us drinks and we sat in a corner.

"Maybe the last pint I'll pull for you," she said, raising her glass.

"Cheers. It won't be the same…"

"…It's been funny sometimes, hasn't it?"

"I'll send you a Scala poster so you can see all the bad films you're missing."

"Thanks. I'll think of you watching them."

She went quiet, twisting her hair.

An arm snaked around my shoulders.

"Billy," breathed Declan, "sorry about your mate, I shouldn't have rapped him."

"He's not really a mate."

"He's a cunt though."

"And you're a savage sometimes," said Jayne.

He stood, swaying slightly, and pointed at his chest.

"Me Declan, you Jayne. What about some drinks for me and Cheetah?"

"Will you help yourself?"

"That's my girl. Here, Max, let's you and me check out the optics."

"All right, but less of the Cheetah."

"So," said Jayne. "Not long now and we're away."

"No, not long, Mrs Doyle."

"Jayne."

"Yeah. Jayne"

Bunkum

There was an early A.M. knock at the door, and there was Joo-Lee, leaning in and looking at me on an angle. Her blank expression quickly shifted into something loose and smiley and she grabbed me close. We remained standing, pressed together in the doorway, for several minutes.

"Billy," she uttered softly, and I thought she was about to cry.

"No, no waterworks," she said.

We went into the living room.

"You really need to redecorate," said Joo-Lee.

She paced the room, prodding at the sagging wallpaper.

"I mean this is so last year. Patterns are out, haven't you heard? Hey, and so am I."

"Sound the alarms."

"Yeah. Look out London town. Blame Max, he somehow convinced them I'm not a total and utter basket case. Well, not all the time."

She tore a strip off the wall and squeezed it into a squishy ball.

"How come I was banged up again, Billy?"

"You just, I don't know, got a bit unwell, I suppose."

"The dreaded unwell woman. Must stop doing that. Hey…"

She threw the paper ball at me.

"Did we, like, get married or anything?"

I tapped my forehead.

"Only in here."

"Cool. I mean, I didn't think so, but my memory's been kind of…interrupted."

Her eyes strayed to the door.

"Listen, Billy, I gotta go. I'm supposed to check in at red camp, or whatever they call it. I guess I'm out on approval."

She blew me a kiss.

"Ciao Billy. We'll hook up soon, right?"

"You know what they say about people who live in glass houses?" asked Brian.

Austin shook his bruised bonce.

"What?"

"They need a hell of a lot of curtains!"

Austin rubbed his eyes.

"I should have gone sick."

He hadn't spoken to me since I arrived for work, which didn't bode well since we were on shift together.

"About Declan…" I began.

"Don't mention that name again. It's history."

This seemed to close the matter, though every time I caught sight of Austin's bandaged brow it was hard to forget.

We had precious little to say to one another, and the shift dragged.

By lunchtime I was chewing at the bit.

I got out and walked down Pentonville road to a little café where I never saw any colleagues. On the way I spotted Maitresse, if that was what she still called herself, standing across the road. She was wearing a shiny plastic mini skirt and an expression of bored indifference, a long cigarette between her lips.

I don't think she noticed me.

By the time I got back, Austin had found his tongue.

"Where were you? I've been stuck with Brenda and Iain. They're a joke, man. Especially her. She can't even have a laugh."

He was obviously still smarting from the attack of the wild elbow woman. (Coming soon to the Scala.)

"It's probably frustration, stupid bitch. She could do with a seeing to. Saying that, who in their right mind would go there? Some people you just can't imagine doing it, know what I'm saying?"

"In Brenda's case I don't need to."

"You and me both, bro."

Knocking off, we beat a familiar path to the Prince of Wales.

Brian was already in, sharing a joke with Bernard.

"Stand by your beds," he said, spotting us. "Here comes the rear guard."

We had barely sat down when in walked Brenda and Iain.

"Blimey!" said Brian. "This is a turn up."

Iain looked uncomfortable, but Brenda was unusually perky, drinking quickly.

"I'll have another," she said. "We'll all have another."

"I'm all right, thank you," said Iain.

Brenda giggled.

"He's all right!"

She raised her glass.

"Bottoms up, boys!"

Brian reddened, spluttering.

"Gone down the wrong way, has it?" asked Iain, slapping him on the back.

"Something like that."

He lit a cigarette and took a deep drag.

"I thought you were off those?" said Iain.

"So did I, mate, so did I."

"Waste of money," said Brenda. "Think how much you could save. Buy yourself something nice."

"I'm thinking of getting myself a bike," said Austin.

"Why not borrow Billy's?" teased Brian.

"No, man, I'm not talking push bikes. I mean a bike, motor cycle, a Harley for instance."

"How exciting," said Brenda. "Would you give me a ride?"

"Might."

"Dangerous hobby," remarked Iain.

Austin shook his head.

"Not if you know how to handle it."

"Apparently you have to lean with the rider," said Brenda.

Iain got up.

"I need an early night. You want a lift, Brenda?"

"Oh, all right."

"Don't force yourself."

"I should go too," I said.

"Riding home?" asked Brian.

When I got back, there was something different. A bag of rubbish leaned against the hall wall. A book on the floor.

Jim came slowly out of Max's room. His eyes were red, and I could see beyond him that the room had been almost cleared.

"They've gone," he said.

"What?"

"Left a note, couldn't tell me to my face."

"Who?"

"Max. He's gone to the States. Him and Joo-Lee. Getting married."

I went to my room, half expecting there might be a note for me too.

Just an old Asti bottle, little bar flies hovering around the neck. I threw it through the hole in the window that Joo-Lee had made, but I got the wrong window.

Two holes now, his and hers.

Jim called up the stairs.

"Will you join me in an Eccles cake? Some people turn to drink, drugs, too many ciggies, I do Eccles cakes."

We sat in the kitchen and he gave me a sad smile.

"This is fairly remarkable even by Max's standards," I said.

"Vintage! No warning, no explanation, just a scribble on one of those office bloody stick-on yellow things."

"Where did he stick it?"

"On the fridge. I know where I'd like to stick it."

"The note or the fridge?"

He coughed on crumbs.

"You're a sweet boy. Tell me, do you ever feel, I don't know, really, really idiotic?"

"Who, me?"

"I think you probably know just how I'm feeling right now."

"Maybe. Didn't Max and you have plans?"

"Plans? Seems like Max was the one with the plans. Trouble is, they didn't include me. How could he carry on as if everything was normal? I think he must be schizophrenic or something."

"Maybe it's catching."

"Joo-Lee, you mean? Not exactly a stable girl. Sorry, you and her were an item, weren't you?"

"Sounds like something on a shelf."

"Which is exactly where I'll end up at this rate. She wasn't the one for you then?"

"So it seems."

"I thought Max was. Just shows you. God, Billy, Max and Joo-Lee!"

"I know. Mr and Mrs Subotsky."

"Don't! I give them a month."

"If that."

He laughed through his tears.

"God, Billy, look at the state of me."

"I see you've packed."

"What little there was. I can't stay here, no offence. Have to move on. Pick myself up. It won't be the first time."

"Will you carry on as Lola?"

"Carry on Lola. Oh, you bet. From now on it's just me and her."

"Now who's schizoid?"

He smiled, brushing crumbs from his shirt.

"I suppose this is goodbye."

He got up and squeezed my arm.

"You take care, Billy, you're going to be all right, you hear me?"

"I hear."

"Good. Which reminds me, Jayne dropped by looking for you."

"Here?"

"Yeah. She said to tell you there's this guy Declan knows has a room going. Like she said, these squats won't last forever."

He handed me a scrap of paper on which Jayne had scribbled a contact number and the name Edwin.

"You better go and call, before it's gone!"

He gave me a hug.

"So long."

Edwin had a maisonette on a council estate in Peckham.

"Come over with your stuff," he said.

I just got the address before the pips went.

I started sorting out my few belongings, sniffing and snotting through the shivery onset of a cold.

One of Liz's socks turned up in a drawer. Day-Glo yellow. I rolled it up and threw it for the cat, but he ignored it and tried to climb into the 'Wavy Line' cardboard box with my stuff.

When I carried him downstairs and put him out, he tried to push back in past the closing door.

"Move into the ambulance," I said through the letterbox.

I picked up my box and looked around the bedroom. The bed was past it, wardrobe too big to move. My drums would have to come later.

When I got to the new flat, box in arms, a woman wearing a headscarf and dressing gown answered the door.

I mentioned the room.

Without a word she went back inside, there was some shouting, and she returned.

"Edwin has no right going offering no rooms," she said, smiling through thin lips. "I'm his mother, and," her voice sank to a bad breath whisper, "he ain't quite, you know…"

I carried the box back to the squat, where the cat was waiting at the door.

"It's you and me, kid," I said, as he hurried in ahead of me.

The Last Supper

Since my aborted attempt to abandon squat, the cat had developed a neurotic habit of following me around, pawing for affection. The fact that he was losing control of his bodily functions made it hard to give.

His mind seemed to be going too. He couldn't, or wouldn't understand the intended function of a cardboard box full of shredded newspaper.

"Crapping not sleeping," I chanted.

He rolled over.

The biscuits I fed him, ('always provide your pet with plenty of fresh water'), claimed to provide a balanced diet. They also provided incredibly bad breath.

It was this that alerted me to his presence one afternoon as I was having a desultory bash on my kit. He was curled up asleep inside the bass drum.

He looked out at me, yawned, and went back to sleep.

Maybe this was the gimmick to rocket 'the Adults' to fame?

I laid down my sticks for the sake of his ears, and went to the Hope.

Bob was at the helm.

"No replacement for Jayne yet?" I asked.

He smiled ruefully.

"They aren't exactly queuing up. I don't suppose you want a job?"

He looked surprised when I told him I had one.

"Girls like Jayne are hard to find," he said, reaching down a glass. "You don't appreciate what you've got till it's gone."

"When are they off?"

"Later today, I think. I'm stuck here till closing, I know that much."

I took my beer to a table near the fire. It was out, grey ashes cold in the grate. They blew up into a little snow scene as someone opened the door.

"Why the long face?" said Declan.

He strode over, rubbing his hands together, followed by Jayne.

"Thought we might find you in here," she said.

"It wouldn't take a genius," added Declan. "What are you having?"

"You're buying me a drink?"

"Call it a goodbye prezzie."

He went over and slapped his palms on the bar.

Jayne sat opposite me, toying with an unravelling thread on the sleeve of her dress.

"Thanks for the tip about the room," I said.

"Sorry?"

"The flat in Peckham."

"Oh, yeah. How was it?"

"Yeah, good."

"You'll be moving on?"

"Yeah, you know. Things don't last forever."

"I suppose they don't."

Declan set three pints on the table.

"Bob let us have 'em on the house."

"Not something I make a habit of," said Bob. "But since you're leaving. You are still going I take it?"

"Try stopping us," said Declan. "Come on, Jayne, drink up. We don't have much time."

She poured some of her beer into mine, and they got up.

Declan glanced around the bar.

"Ah, well, this is it. Cheers Billy."

He mock punched my arm.

"Good luck," I said.

He nodded, took a last lingering look at the fire, and turned towards the door.

Jayne held out her arms.

"You take care," she said quietly.

Her threadbare dress trailed behind her as she walked away.

I woke from a dream of Declan setting fire to a giant wooden chair.

My alarm clock wasn't working and I'd slept late. Couldn't be bothered to go looking for an un-vandalised 'phone box in order to call sick.

I went into the kitchen, and as I was washing a cup, realised I was standing in a pool of urine. The cat slunk out.

Boiling water for tea, I found there was only dust in the caddie. I turned off the gas and went out.

There was thin sunlight and a chill breeze off the river.

I struck out south, Surrey Docks, South Bermondsey, Nunhead, and climbed the steps to the top of One Tree Hill. From there the City lay exposed before me, a compressed panorama. St Paul's, Guy's hospital, Post Office Tower, Tower bridge.

And down river, squashed in among it all, the squat.

A man walked by with his dog, and paused, shading his eyes.

"Lovely, isn't it?" he said.

I walked slowly home, and stood for a moment, observing the building I lived in.

Most of the windows were broken, gutters cracked and rusting. Doors hanging off their hinges. Fallen tiles.

I went in, and as I pushed the door an envelope rustled across the mat.

It was addressed to Joo-Lee, no return address, and contained a brief scribble from her father, folded around two clean, flat fifty pound notes.

Boozeroo

Money in my pocket, but I just ain't got no love.
Pint of best and a double Scotch.
Hold the ice.
I'm doing lengths in the drowning pool of sorrows.
Someone breaks in and steals my snare. Like I care.
In the post, a photo of Max and Joo-Lee. He's wearing a top hat. Is that an orange blossom in her hair?
I'm gonna find me a river, one that's made of beer.
Going down in it three times, coming up twice for air.
I take to wearing an old pair of Joo-Lee's sunglasses. She used to call them her shades of Bacchus.
Peering through them at a barman as he examines the fifty note I gave him.
"Where's your white stick?" says an old man.
Peters and Joo-Lee.
His nose, knotted with blue, inhabits my dreams for nights.
"Thinks the world owes him a living."
A feckless shit with folding stuff to fritter, brace of Grouse and a pint of bitter.
 "Set 'em up, same again."
"I think you've had enough."
"Fuck you very much."
The world outside looks over-exposed.
Albion Street.
Hey, hey, wait a minute! Far off figure in a cap, coming my way. Is it?
My pace quickens, but I have to check my smile when we pass. Postmen are definitely getting younger. He eyes me, gripping his bag.
"Nothing for me then?"
Return to sender.
There are dry leaves in my turn-ups, and I don't think I've been home for a while.
How long?
Headlong.

One drab afternoon, a haulage truck trundling past the pub window, Nik Kershaw on the juke, a window cleaner, lollypop lady, kids carrying homework, postman, potman, woman pushing a pram, the person pulling my pint.

King's Cross.
I smuggle something sinister in to the Scala. Actually, just a little innocent bottle of spirits.
The programme is 'Wild Westerns.' 'Johnny Guitar', 'The Outlaw', 'Terror in a Texas Town'.
Sterling Hayden bites his lip.
"People are just like any other kind of animal," someone tells him. "When they're scared, they scatter."
Cold air flushes the Scala fug as I step out.
Hey, I'm in Prince of Wales territory, and there's a one-in-seven chance it's Thursday.
And there they are, Brian and Bernard at the bar, laughing.
"Well look who it isn't," says Brian.

His smile dissolves as I weave my way over.

"Christ, he's totally shickered," he whispers to Bernard, who nods and won't serve me.

I get out the rum.

"Come on, mate," says Brian, putting his arm round my shoulders. "What's the story?"

Austin comes out from the toilet. His leg's in plaster, and he's hobbling on crutches.

"He got that motorbike, then?" I say.

Brian laughs.

"Hello, stranger," says Austin, " what's the joke?"

I almost fall against him.

"Careful, man! I'm injured, in case you didn't notice."

Bernard lets me sit with them.

"The bottle stays in your pocket."

It does. Except when I'm in the gents.

Brian's getting lushed.

"Go on, mate, cop a feel."

Austin's gone.

"It's like a pole."

I'm gone.

Grays Inn Road, take me home.

Water Rats. Late licence.

Steep kerb.

Pavement.

Mooncalf

The sun came through the blind, sending slats of light across the poster of Cary Grant

and Randolph Scott on the wall.

I heard voices, footsteps approaching, and tried to raise my head from the feather-soft pillow. Scintillating spangles of light burst and scattered in front of my eyes, causing me to sink back. I lay mesmerised as they continued to sparkle and fade.

There was a knock, and Peter peered round the door.

"Are you decent?"

"Is he alive, more to the point?" added Joe, following him in and placing a tray by the bed.

"We hedged our bets and brought you coffee, orange juice and water," said Peter.

Joe sat on the bed.

"We found you on our way back from the Bell."

"Nearly didn't stop," said Peter. "Then I recognised my watch. 'That's my old Seiko,' I said, didn't I Joe?"

He nodded.

"We could hardly leave it lying in the gutter, could we?"

I drank some water.

"Quite the good Samaritans, weren't we?" said Peter. "Oh, look, I have to dash."

He patted the duvet.

"You try to look after yourself a bit better."

He kissed Joe and hurried out.

"So, how're you feeling?" asked Joe, with a wry grin.

"I've been worse."

"Really?"

"You look very well, anyway."

"Yeah. Peter's great. Asked me to move in with him, so I gave up my flat. How's the squat? Max still winding you up?"

"In a sense."

"Don't suppose you ever see anything of Alison? I can hardly believe I was with her so long. Lucky escape."

"Everyone's escaping."

"Eh?"

"Oh, Jayne and Declan, off to Ireland, Mr and Mrs."

"Never! Joo-Lee still around?"

"I'll tell you all about it some time."

"Yeah, sorry, talking too much. My bath'll be running over."

He skipped out, and I managed to sit up.

My jacket was hanging on the end of the bed. In the pockets were three crumpled pound notes, a broken cigarette, ticket for the number 88 bus, a condom sealed in worn foil, and a small quantity of white dust in a little polythene bag.

Joe came back in with a towel round him.

"I didn't know you did speed," he remarked.

"Neither did I."

He dipped his finger in the bag and sucked it.

"Ooh, nasty. I wouldn't if I were you. I've got a spot of the real deal if you're interested."

"No, thanks. I think I have to start getting myself together."

He waved from an upstairs window as I walked away.

Back home, mail rustled across the hall as I opened the door. The air was cold and damp in the silent squat.

I suddenly remembered the cat, and hurried upstairs. The bass drum was empty. Went over and looked through the broken window. Cool air blew in, disturbing some wisps of fur caught on the jagged glass. Big cat had cut loose.

He had the right idea.

My stuff was still packed in a box. I just had to pick it up and walk.

First, a quick one in the Hope. A decider.

But the door was boarded and barred.

I returned to the squat and started picking through the post. Mostly junk. Flyer for a take-away called Tin Luk, featuring vegetarian beef chow mein. Reminder of Max putting his foot in it. Offers of credit cards and loans. A leaflet, 'let me destroy your problems before they destroy you. Mr Nadir, genuine spiritual healer. If your wife, husband, lover gone, I can restore them…'

I went into the kitchen to make tea, but there was no tea, and the milk was sour. Switched on the radio, and the Archers theme almost drowned out a rap at the letterbox. I turned down the volume and went quietly into the hall, wary of official visitors.

Through the dirty, wired glass was the shape of someone bending to the letterbox, sound of a female voice.

"Billy?"

I opened the door.

"God, Billy, where've you been?" said Jayne. "You scared the bejasus out of me." She had a bag with her.

"I've everything I own in here! Hey, didn't you get my notes? I've been round here that many times, and all I could hear was that bloody cat. It's really good to see you."

"And you. But what about Ireland? Declan?"

"Ah, the poor fool. I couldn't go through with it, Billy. We got as far as Rhyll and I just had to get off the train and come back."

"Does it stop at Rhyll?"

"It does if you pull the emergency chord. God, Declan was cursing."

"He must have been pretty upset."

"Well, he had Theresa, you know, that wee dog, and he reckoned he could sell my boat ticket at Holyhead."

"Adaptable, isn't he?"

"No kidding. He might at least have blubbed. You know what, though? I don't think he ever really believed it was going to happen any more than I did."

"So what now?"

"That's what I've been wanting to tell you. I've a brother in New Orleans manages a bar. He reckons he can get me a job."

"Well there's nothing left round here. Did you see the Hope?"

"I know. End of an era. Probably just as well."

"I hope the Deep South suits you."

She looked at her feet, then up again, smiling.

"Why don't you come with me? There's loads of bands and bars. You could play the drums. It'll be great!"

Written by Chris Fenner.

Printed in Great Britain
by Amazon

38817663R00072